DEATH FOR OLD TIME'S SAKE

Last night Canyon O'Grady and Paddy McNamara had had quite a reunion. A lot of red-eye had gone down their throats as they talked about water gone under the bridge.

This morning things were different.

McNamara stood in front of Canyon, his right hand hovering over the six-gun on his hip.

"O'Grady! You double-crossing son-of-a-bitch!" McNamara spat out. "What kind of back-stabber have you turned into? Hell, it don't matter none, because in about ten seconds, you're gonna be dead. Go for your leather, O'Grady. You're dead already, you just don't know it."

With a friend like McNamara, Canyon didn't need enemies—though he had a helluva lot of those, too . . .

JON SHARPE'S WILD WEST

☐ **CANYON O'GRADY #1: DEAD MEN'S TRAILS by Jon Sharpe.** Meet Canyon O'Grady, a government special agent whose only badge, as he rides the roughest trails in the West, is the colt in his holster. O'Grady quickly learns that dead men tell no tales, and live killers show no mercy as he hunts down the slayer of the great American hero Merriwether Lewis.
(160681—$2.95)

☐ **CANYON O'GRADY #2: SILVER SLAUGHTER by Jon Sharpe.** With a flashing grin and a blazing gun, Canyon O'Grady rides the trail of treachery, greed, and gore in search of nameless thieves who are stealing a vital stream of silver bullion from the U.S. government. (160703—$2.95)

☐ **CANYON O'GRADY #3: MACHINE GUN MADNESS by Jon Sharpe.** A gun was invented that spat out bullets faster than a man could blink and every malcontent in the Union wanted it. Canyon's job was to ride the most savage crossfire the West had ever seen to rescue the deadliest weapon the world had ever known. (161521—$2.95)

☐ **CANYON O'GRADY #4: SHADOW GUNS by Jon Sharpe.** With America split between North and South and Missouri being a border state both sides wanted, Canyon O'Grady finds himself in a crossfire of doublecross trying to keep a ruthless pro-slavery candidate from using bullets to win a vital election. (162765—$3.50)

☐ **CANYON O'GRADY #5: THE LINCOLN ASSIGNMENT by Jon Sharpe.** Bullets, not ballots, were Canyon O'Grady's business as top frontier trouble-shooter for the U.S. Government. But now he was tangled up in election intrigue, as he tried to stop a plot aimed at keeping Abe Lincoln out of office by putting him in his grave. (163680—$3.50)

Buy them at your local bookstore or use this convenient coupon for ordering.

NEW AMERICAN LIBRARY
P.O. Box 999, Bergenfield, New Jersey 07621

Please send me the books I have checked above. I am enclosing $_____ (please add $1.00 to this order to cover postage and handling). Send check or money order— no cash or C.O.D.'s. Prices and numbers are subject to change without notice.

Name_____

Address_____

City _____ State _____ Zip _____
Allow 4-6 weeks for delivery.
This offer, prices and numbers are subject to change without notice.

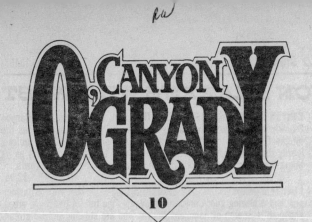

CANYON O'GRADY

10

THE GREAT LAND SWINDLE

by
Jon Sharpe

A SIGNET BOOK

SIGNET
Published by the Penguin Group
Penguin Books USA Inc., 375 Hudson Street,
New York, New York 10014, U.S.A.
Penguin Books Ltd, 27 Wrights Lane,
London W8 5TZ, England
Penguin Books Australia Ltd, Ringwood,
Victoria, Australia
Penguin Books Canada Ltd, 2801 John Street,
Markham, Ontario, Canada L3R 1B4
Penguin Books (N.Z.) Ltd, 182-190 Wairau Road,
Auckland 10, New Zealand

Penguin Books Ltd, Registered Offices:
Harmondsworth, Middlesex, England

First published by Signet, an imprint of New American Library, a division of
Penguin Books USA Inc.

First Printing, November 1990
10 9 8 7 6 5 4 3 2 1

Canyon O'Grady

His was a heritage of blackguards and poets, fighters and lovers, men who could draw a pistol and bed a lass with the same ease.

Freedom was a cry seared into Canyon O'Grady, justice a banner of his heart.

With the great wave of those who fled to America, the new land of hope and heartbreak, solace and savagery, he came to ride the untamed wildness of the Old West.

With a smile or a six-gun, Canyon O'Grady became a name feared by some and welcomed by others, but remembered by all. . . .

*Is Canyon O'Grady's boyhood friend
a part of a tremendous land swindle,
or is he a victim of circumstances?
Will it all work out in friendship or
in a blazing shootout between
Canyon and his friend?*

1

Canyon O'Grady sat on the palomino and looked across the last little rise outside Santa Fe. The air was so clear that the little town cradled between the four mountain ranges had the look of an early Spanish painting.

He lifted his wide-brimmed gray hat and wiped sweat from his forehead. Even at an altitude of more than seven thousand feet the air was hot and dry this August afternoon. Canyon was letting Cormac rest as much as he was allowing himself a pause. The horse had been working hard the last three miles and he was in no big rush. His work was done twenty miles to the west. He had to make one last stop in Santa Fe before buying a ticket on the eastbound stage and heading out on the Santa Fe trail for St. Louis then the long ride back to Washington, D.C.

He liked the smell of the ponderosa pines that covered this far end of the great Rocky Mountain Range. He took a deep breath, and nudged the palomino down the trail. He should be in Santa Fe well before dark.

It was only a little after five o'clock when he tied his horse outside La Conchita, the best restaurant in the old Spanish section of Santa Fe. He slapped his hat on his pants and shirt to get off some of the trail dust. He had taken a room at the hotel nearby and now went inside the café and found a table.

Here you didn't order. A waiter brought a big mug of beer. Later he served Canyon a huge plate filled with refried beans and a half a dozen rolled tortillas stuffed with meat, hot peppers, and cheese.

He had almost finished his meal when he saw a man at an adjoining table watching him. Canyon's right hand relaxed and dropped near his right thigh to be close to the tied down Colt .45 that rested there.

Canyon watched the stranger a moment before the man grinned and stood. He came directly toward Canyon's table. The tall man eased to his feet, his gun hand still close to iron.

"I'll be a son of a bitch," the stranger said. "If you ain't Canyon O'Grady, you're sure his twin brother."

Canyon tensed more. The man was smiling. But he remembered an outlaw in Wyoming who always smiled grandly when he killed someone.

The man stopped four feet from Canyon, his grin broader now. "Damn, got to be Canyon O'Grady. With that red hair and that ugly face, who else could it be?" The man paused. He was four inches under six feet, broad-shouldered, looked fit, and had the white face of a man not out in the weather or wind much. His hands were clean, and so were his fingernails. He was slender, well-dressed, and had a sturdy mustache squared off on the ends. The man chuckled. "You still don't remember me, do you, Canyon?"

The stranger lifted one hand and grinned. "Hey, relax, I'm friendly. I'm not gunning for you, ease up there, old man. I knew you when we both were snot-nosed kids about ten or twelve. Remember Almont Street in Brooklyn?''

Canyon looked at the man closer now, memories flooding back.

"Paddy?" Canyon asked.

"Damn, you do remember. Yeah. Paddy McNamara, Rooster McNamara's oldest. We lived two houses down from you on the same side of the street.''

"Be damned," Canyon said. He held out his hand and the other man shook it. "Don't think I would have recognized you, Paddy, if you hadn't mentioned Almont Street. Hell, you're twice as ugly as you were then.''

They both laughed.

"Sit down," Canyon said. "Finished your supper?''

"Just did. What the hell you doing in a down-in-the-mouth place like Santa Fe, Canyon?''

"Passing through, mostly. Planning on grabbing the stage in a day or two and heading out for St. Louis.''

Paddy McNamara motioned with one of his hands. "You all finished eating?''

"Enough, I guess.''

"Good. Let's find a saloon and I'll buy you a couple of drinks. I got an idea to hit you with.''

"What sort?''

"Not worth mentioning until we have at least three beers.''

They went to the first saloon down the boardwalk and ordered beers and took the frothy mugs to a table near the wall. For half an hour they remembered trouble they had been in as two kids in Brooklyn.

They had downed four beers each when Paddy bought a bottle of whiskey and brought two glasses to the table. They worked on the whiskey for a while, but Paddy drank twice what Canyon did. At last Paddy got around to his news.

"Canyon, old friend, in three days I got a little job to do for a friend. All I have to do is meet the stage coming down the trail from Albuquerque and stop it about five miles south of town. I'm looking for a few men to help me do it."

"Stop the stage?" Canyon repeated. "What for?"

"Didn't ask. When some slick gent offers me two hundred dollars in gold just to stop a stage, hell, it's gonna get stopped. The stage from the south gets into town about four in the afternoon. So we stop it about three. Ain't figured out how, yet."

Canyon stared at his years ago best friend. He'd had a few drinks, but he wasn't so drunk that he'd forgotten that stopping a stage with mail on board was a federal crime. A man could get a year in jail for doing that.

"You ain't gonna rob the strongbox, are you?" Canyon asked.

"Hell, no! Not with just a couple of men and not five miles from town. I might be dumb, but I'm not that stupid. Don't know why Arch wants the stage stopped. He just said to stop the damn thing. So, hell, we'll stop it, then we all run like a bitch."

"Sounds fishy as hell," Canyon said. "Whole thing sounds fishy as all get-out. Why does somebody want to stop the stage so close in? Did this Arch say why?"

Paddy drained the last of the whiskey in his glass. "He didn't. Said it was none of my damned business. Bet if we get him drunk, he'd tell us. Let's go find him."

Canyon thought for a moment about tracking Arch down now. But he'd had more to drink than he should have in order to handle a confrontation well. And Paddy was too drunk to be relied on. "No, no, not me," he responded. "I'm too damn tired. Going to get some sleep."

Paddy stared at his old friend, then nodded. "That's a good idea. You're drunk."

Canyon just smiled and stood. It took three tries to get Paddy to his feet.

"What's the name of your hotel?"

Paddy stared at him, shook his head. "Huh. Damned if I know. Near the restaurant."

Canyon helped Paddy out of the saloon and along the boardwalk to the eatery.

At the third hotel they tried the room clerk grinned at them and said Paddy was in Room 12. Canyon helped him up the stairs and down the hall to his room.

"I'll see you tomorrow, old friend," Paddy said. "Got to convince you to help me."

Canyon returned to his own room. Without taking off his shirt or even his boots, he smashed into sleep and didn't wake up until well past dawn the next morning.

The room was light, but it took Canyon five minutes to realize that he was alive. He had mixed too much booze last night. Paddy McNamara. Be damned. Hadn't even thought of the short, tough little kid for ten years. They used to be best friends, got in and out of more kid trouble than you could shake a stick at. Damn but those were fun days.

Canyon sat up at last and tried to still the big gong pounding in his head. He grinned, thinking about how Paddy must feel. A good hot cup of coffee usually ruined a hangover. He washed, dressed, brushed off his hat, and headed down to the street. Half a block down he saw a sign that said BREAKFAST 25 CENTS. He walked in and sat down.

"Eggs or flapjacks?" a voice asked him. He looked up to find a smiling pretty girl with a stub pencil poised over a pad of paper. She had the biggest brown eyes he had ever seen set in a cute round face framed by jet-black hair. She grinned at him.

"Three eggs sunnyside up, two flapjacks, a batch of country-fried potatoes, toast, and coffee," Canyon said.

The girl hesitated, staring directly into his eyes for a moment. Then she smiled and turned away. Her full breasts swung against the thin blouse and at last decided to go with her.

By the time the breakfast came Canyon had reviewed his conversation with Paddy. Paddy had been hired by Arch somebody to stop the stage. Why stop a stagecoach outside the town? The most obvious answer was to rob it. But Paddy wasn't a robber, or so he said. Why else? Kidnap someone? Kill a passenger? He thought it through as he finished his breakfast. He needed to talk to the sheriff. Without knowing who this Arch might be, Canyon couldn't even try to anticipate his motives.

He went up to the counter, paid his quarter for the meal, and gave the waitress a dime tip. That brought him a large smile.

"Thanks," she said. "My name's Jill. Hope you'll come in again."

"I will. Name's Canyon O'Grady."

"Canyon? Interesting name. Nice to meet you, Canyon O'Grady."

"Well, Jill, nice to meet you as well. Might see you later."

Canyon found the sheriff's office after a short search and soon had a private meeting with Luke Parrish, sheriff of Santa Fe County.

Briefly Canyon laid out his chance meeting with an old friend and the proposition.

"An interesting situation," the sheriff replied. "Why are you so damn concerned."

Canyon took out his wallet and extracted a thin, closely printed card. On it was glued a small tintype photo of Canyon. The card said that Canyon O'Grady was a special agent of the U.S. government on assignment by President James Buchanan. "All cooperation is expected by local, county, and state law-enforcement agencies and officials." The card was signed by President Buchanan.

Sheriff Parrish read the card a second time, checked the picture against Canyon, and handed it back. "Well, now. I've never seen one of those cards before. Must not be many of you. I can see why you were concerned."

"Stopping a stage coach carrying U.S. mail is a federal offense. And almost all stages carry mail these days. But first I need to ask, who is this Arch?"

"That could be a problem. The first man I think of is Archibald Forester, one of our local politicians. He's ambitious and not beyond stretching the law a bit here and there for his own benefit. He's one of the most powerful men in the territory."

The sheriff snapped his fingers. "Three days from yesterday makes it the fourteenth. I had a letter here somewhere about the fourteenth. Where was it?" He looked around his desk a minute, then grabbed a sheet of paper.

"Yeah. On the fourteenth, we're having some visitors. I'm supposed to be sure to present some security at the stage depot for the four P.M. arrival of our territorial governor, along with the junior United States senator from Iowa."

"So important people are arriving and Archibald Forester wants the stage stopped outside of town? Sounds ominous to me, Sheriff."

"Damn ominous." Parrish lit a pipe he'd been tamping full of tobacco. "You on assignment right now, Canyon?"

"Just finished one. I was going to head east this afternoon. But now I might stay around for a while. Help you find out what's going on. I could send a letter to my office and tell them I'm needed here for a while. I might be able to help out."

"Well, if you have the time. If Archibald Forester is mixed up in this, I could use some help."

Canyon asked the sheriff to telegraph General Wheeler that he would be delayed. Parrish agreed, and that settled, Canyon walked out the front door. And almost collided with Paddy McNamara.

"Canyon! You double-crossing son of a bitch! What the hell were you doing talking to Parrish?" He backed up slowly, his right hand hovering over a six-gun on his hip that Canyon saw was tied down low. "You told the sheriff everything, didn't you, O'Grady? What kind of a back-stabber have you turned into? It doesn't matter none, because in about ten seconds you're gonna be dead."

Canyon knew there was nothing else he could do.

He saw the other man's hand dart upward, hitting the butt of his revolver, starting its upward movement. With a touch of sadness and regret, Canyon reached for the deadly .45 six-gun in his holster.

2

Canyon began his draw. His right hand came up, caught the rough handle of the .45, lifted it with his three lower fingers until it was high enough that his trigger finger could slide into the trigger guard.

As this was happening, his right thumb connected with the hammer and he drew it back until it clicked into place. By that time the muzzle had cleared the leather holster, and instead of continuing upward, Canyon's hand pushed the weapon out forward and he sighted with the weapon as he would by pointing his finger.

All of this took a mere fraction of a second and the Colt in his hand roared as his finger stroked the trigger. Even as the big gun bucked, his thumb drew back the hammer again, spinning the cylinder to the next unfired round and locking the hammer back ready for the second shot.

Canyon saw his first round rip into Paddy McNamara's right side and jolt him backward a half-step. The hit came just as Paddy was starting to fire. He couldn't stop his finger. The weapon discharged as he smashed backward and his gun hand jolted the weapon to the right well off target as the hammer fell.

The force of the round slammed Paddy three feet to the rear and dropped him onto the hard planks of the boardwalk. His .44 bounced from his hand and skittered away from his outstretched fingers.

Before Canyon could react, the sheriff's office door burst open and the lawman stood there with a shotgun in both hands, the double barrels ready to blast.

"Hold it, both of you," Parrish bellowed. He looked fiercely at Canyon, decided that the redhead would hold his fire, then squatted beside Paddy.

"Looks like you caught some lead in your side, young man. Suggest we get you over to see Doc Holtzman."

Paddy let the sheriff help him up and glared at Canyon. "I can get over there myself, Sheriff. I want to charge that man with attempted murder."

"I heard two shots and your weapon's been fired. Sounds like a fair fight to me. Move on over to Doc's and get patched up. You can pick up your gun at the office later."

Parrish dispersed the small crowd that had gathered, then waved Canyon into the office. Inside the sheriff closed the door and scowled.

"Not smart, O'Grady, letting him see you come out of my place. You best watch your back with him in town. Forester was mayor once. A lot of people here owe him favors and plenty more wouldn't mind it if Archibald Forester had reason to look kindly on them. If your friend lets him know what's happened, somebody may decide to put a hole in you."

"Dandy. Can you give me the name of a man who knows the local politics who's also honest and we can trust?"

"Try Professor Offenhauser. He used to teach at Harvard University. Retired out here for his health a dozen years ago."

Canyon got Offenhauser's address and directions to the house.

"One more thing, Sheriff. I suggest you either send a man to Albuquerque or send a strongly worded message to the U.S. senator and his party advising them not to take the stage on the fourteenth."

Sheriff Parrish stared out the window at the street. "We don't know for sure what was planned for the fourteenth. I'd rather not get the senator upset if we can handle this here."

"I can understand that, but don't count on it. Maybe you should have one of your men on the stage with a sawed-off shotgun."

Parrish grinned. "O'Grady, I'm starting to like the way you think. I'll put one of my deputies on board and suggest that the senator also brings an Albuquerque lawman up here with him as an armed escort."

Canyon went out the back door of the jail and headed for Professor Offenhauser's house.

Twenty minutes later, Canyon sat in the parlor of the Offenhauser home. The professor, in his seventies, was small and stooped. He wheezed a little when he spoke, but his blue eyes were bright and clear.

"Forester is a jackass," Offenhauser said. "He wanted to be territorial governor, but Buchanan wouldn't buy it. The president appoints the officials to help a new territory get started. I think Buchanan knew Forester was more interested in filling his pockets than in turning New Mexico into a state.

"Let me tell you about Archibald Forester. He grew

up here. His father owned three businesses, did a lot of early-day trading and teamstering. The old man made a lot of money. Archibald inherited it all about ten years ago and has multiplied that small fortune into a larger one. He has three children, all boys.

"The man wanted to be governor. Buchanan appointed someone else, so now Forester's concentrating on being as big a pistol as he can in the territorial legislature."

"How are his business practices? Honest?"

"When he has to be. He's been in on some legal but not very charitable foreclosures and some other slick deals most men would not touch. He's never been arrested or even charged with anything illegal."

"He has a hidden dark side to him?"

"Hell, we all have that. Forester doesn't seem to show much of his, though. No, he doesn't run with a pack of wolves, if that's what you're asking. Church man, local charities, business association, all the right clubs."

"Is Forester a good friend of the governor's?"

"Opposite sides of the political fence. Been some spirited exchanges between the two. Just offhand, I'd say Forester is jealous as hell of Governor Taggart."

Canyon told Offenhauser about the plan by Forester for stopping the stage. "What do you make of this, Professor, since evidently the plot originated with Forester?"

"Damn peculiar."

"Your first belly reaction, Professor."

"That somebody is going to get killed."

"Who?"

"Not Forester, for damn sure. Which leaves the

governor and the senator. Clark Jamison is from Iowa. I hear about him from time to time. He is not the best senator in that august body. Either one could be the target.''

"So where does that leave us?" Canyon asked.

"Changing the schedule of the senator and governor."

"Been done by the sheriff."

The older man looked at Canyon closely. "So why are you involved in this, Mr. O'Grady?"

"I'm not really sure yet. Just curious, maybe. I'm going to do some thinking on it. If you hear anything Archibald Forester is up to, I'd appreciate knowing about it. I'm staying at the Blue Spruce Hotel.''

"Good luck and be careful, young man. This is a civilized community compared to many out here in the West, but still we have a few who think it's a wild wilderness.''

Canyon shook hands with the professor, who insisted on getting up and showing him to the door of the small and sparkling clean house. There was a woman's touch here, but Canyon didn't see anyone else in the house.

O'Grady walked down the street toward town. Twice he checked behind. No one followed him. He walked wide around corners and looked carefully into the two alleys that he crossed before he came to the sheriff's office. He went in the back door, which was opened after he knocked.

The sheriff was helpful in answering Canyon's questions.

"Forester lives at 124 Alomar Lane. That's about eight blocks from here, near the new temporary statehouse. He often works out of an office on Paseo de Peralta, two blocks over. It's an adobe building painted white with a bright-red door. Can't miss it.'' The lawman grinned. ''You going over for a chat?''

''Not likely. What does he look like?''

''About five-eight, stocky. Always wears a western hat with a China pheasant feather in it. Hard man to miss. Likes red vests. You looking for him?''

''I figured I might watch his place awhile and see if I could get a feel for the man, what he does, where he goes. You get a man off to Albuquerque?''

''Sure as hell.''

''Good. I'm going to ride along the stage road and see who I can see arriving for the party. Even if Paddy tells Forester that I came to see you, they'll still have to stop the stage. We'll see what happens.''

''My man on board is Shorty Barlow. He'll have the scattergun, so don't draw down on him.''

''No chance.'' Canyon left by the back door again, passed down the alley, and came out a block from the street he was looking for. He spotted the white building with the red door. In the shadow of a wooden building across the street he pulled his hat down over his eyes, leaving enough room to watch the place.

Canyon stood there for nearly an hour before the red door opened. Three men came out, none of them was Paddy or Forester. He waited another hour, hoping the man would come out for a noon meal. He didn't.

Canyon gave up a half-hour later and returned to the café where he had breakfast.

Jill saw him come in and brought him a handwritten menu. Her brown dark eyes glistened as she watched him.

The stew was good and there was home-made jam for the thick slices of toast. He made small talk with the waitress for a while, then paid his twenty cents at the counter.

"Supper is from five to eight," she told him. "Then I close up. Why don't you come by?"

She was busy at the counter then and Canyon went out the front door after a quick look up and down the boardwalk. He thought of trying to find Paddy, but that might be impossible. There were a dozen saloons he could see and as many *cantinas* where Paddy might be hiding.

Canyon returned to watching the red door. A few men went in and came out, but none of them was stocky or wore a red vest or a western hat with a pheasant feather in it.

It was well after three that afternoon when O'Grady gave up and went to the livery where he had left his big palomino stallion, Cormac. He made sure he had a feeding of oats and hay and brushed him down. The next afternoon he would need him to ride south on the Albuquerque trail.

He had just paid the hostler for another two days' board for the horse and started out the door when three men pushed in the wide door shoulder to shoulder. Paddy stood in the middle; the six-gun in his right hand was aimed directly at Canyon O'Grady.

"Well, well, well. If it ain't Canyon O'Grady from Brooklyn," McNamara said.

One of the men grabbed Canyon's revolver and the other crowded him to the rear.

Paddy's voice was menacing.

"Yeah, out in back of the stables, that'll be a fine place for our little talk with Mr. O'Grady. At least we'll be talking. He might not be able to say a word when we're through with him."

3

"Not at all what I expected from you, Paddy. A shot in the back from a dark alley would be more your style. What happened, you go soft since we left Brooklyn?" Canyon taunted.

"Not soft enough to go running to the sheriff about our little conversation last night."

"Conversation? That was a bunch of drunken drivel, babble that I don't even remember. I went to see the sheriff this morning because somebody stole my horse. But if somebody draws on me, I go for the hog leg, too. Now I see it's too bad I didn't kill you yesterday and have it over with."

"You got lucky, my sights hung up on leather."

"Sure. Your yellow streak showed, that was your problem. Now you need two trail mates with weak minds to help you. Never happened this way back in Brooklyn. You could fight your own fights then. You're really gone downhill, Paddy."

"Shut up! Your horse wasn't stolen. I saw you rubbing him down about ten minutes ago. You lie easy, O'Grady. But you can't lie your way out of this one. I figure you won't ride far tomorrow with a broken leg and arm and your face beat in."

They had walked through the barn, out the back door, and were now passing the rear corral. One of the big toughs was behind Canyon and one in front of him. He had an idea but didn't know if it would work. He saw Paddy to one side still holding the six-gun.

Canyon took a quick step forward and kicked as hard as he could, slamming his heavy boot upward between the thug's thighs.

His toe smashed high, spreading the man's legs and ramming hard against his pelvic bones. Between boot and bone lay one of the man's testicles. The victim roared in tremendous pain as he fell to the side and curled into a ball.

Canyon hadn't waited to see the effects of the blow. He had already pulled down his foot and spun, and his fist slanted off the rear guard's forehead. The blow blasted the man back a step. Canyon dived for the thug, wrestled him to the ground, and jerked the six-gun from his holster. Holding the man with a half nelson around his neck, Canyon pushed behind him, using him as a shield.

"Drop it, Paddy, or you're a dead man," Canyon barked.

McNamara quickly eyed the barn door ten feet behind him. Canyon was almost entirely protected behind the downed man. It would be impossible to get off a clean shot. Slowly he let his six-gun lower and then tossed it in the dirt.

"Walk away from it."

"Bastard!"

"A lot of folks agree with you. Walk!"

Paddy took half a dozen steps back toward the pasture behind the livery.

"Good, Paddy. You learn fast. Now start running for the pine trees over there. It's only a half-mile. You should be able to make it all the way before you stop. Get moving."

"You shot me in the side. You know that I can't run," Paddy said.

"Hell, you run right now or I'll match that side wound with one on the other side. Run, dammit!" Canyon fired one shot close to his feet and Paddy took off on a respectable trot toward the blue ridge of mountains to the east.

Canyon watched him go. Paddy was less than fifty yards away when he looked back. Canyon put another round near him. He was almost out of range, but Paddy forgot that. He kept running for another hundred yards before he figured he was clear of the revolver. Then he screamed at his tormentor and circled around, heading back to town.

Canyon let the thug he held fall to the ground and nudged him with his toe. "You move for half an hour and I'm going to ventilate your worthless hide with about five rounds from the Spencer carbine I got in my saddle boot. Those fifty-two-caliber slugs make a respectable hole going in and really expand when they come out. Remember that. Next time you want to beat up on somebody, pick on someone as dumb as you are."

Canyon collected his own gun, took both the revolvers the two thugs had carried, and walked away. He spent the next hour watching Archibald Forester's office. He had no thoughts that the important man would do anything out of the ordinary, especially if he had some skulduggery planned.

About four o'clock, he saw the door open and an

28

average-sized man came out. When he turned and came toward Canyon, the agent could see the man was short and fat and wore a bright-red vest and a western hat with a high crown and a multicolored pheasant feather in the band. Had to be Archibald Forester himself.

He let Forester pass and followed him down two blocks, then the former mayor looked around quickly. Canyon stepped behind a buggy when he noticed the man slowing.

In two quick steps, Forester slipped into the alley. Canyon hurried forward, and when he reached the alley, he grinned. The man who wanted to be territorial governor of New Mexico had just hurried down the alley that led to the back doors of four of the biggest bordellos in Santa Fe.

Forester went into the second whorehouse from the end of the block. Canyon made a mental note of it and wandered back to the main street. He tried to decide what else he had to do before his ride in the morning.

He walked back to Jill's Café and sat at the small counter. Jill came out smiling.

"About time you showed up again," she said. "I hope you're hungry." She watched him a minute without trying to cover up the adoration shining in her eyes, then poured him some coffee. "Don't go away, I'll be right back." She hurried back to the kitchen.

It was ten minutes before she came back. She placed in front of him a platter with a large venison steak on it. It was nearly an inch thick and as big as the plate. Two side dishes held cooked peas and carrots, a big plate of mashed potatoes and brown gravy.

It was a great meal. When he finished, she began

clearing his dishes. "I'll be done in a minute," she promised. "Meet me out back."

Canyon walked out the front door of the café, turned to the left, and meandered along the side of the eatery toward the house in back. As he waited, he considered the state of things. The change in Paddy still surprised him. He had been a little wild as a kid, but he hadn't been so violently inclined. Either Canyon's memory was bad, or Paddy had more at risk than it seemed.

Jill came out the back of the café, a big smile on her face. She led the way into the small house. Once inside, she took his hand and drew him through the kitchen to a small bedroom.

She put her hands around his neck and drew his face down so she could kiss him. Her lips devoured his, nibbling him, biting his lips, then capturing his tongue and battling with it with her own. She held him tightly, her breasts pushing hard against his chest. She moaned and kissed him again, her hands fingering his hair, keeping his mouth against hers.

When her lips at last left his, she sighed. "Oh, but I've been dreaming of this, you are so . . . so good!"

Canyon eased away from her and covered one of her breasts with his hand. Slowly he caressed it, around and around, then stroked the growing nipple that showed now through the thin dress she wore.

Jill's breath grew heavy. Her eyes closed and she leaned against his shoulder, pushing her breasts at his hand. "Glory, but you know how to treat a woman. Feels so warm and good, like I don't want you ever to stop." Her breath came in quick gasps.

Her hand reached down and felt his waist, then his

crotch until she found the hardness behind his fly. "Oh, glory," she said softly. "Oh, glory!"

Her eyes turned to him and he saw them burning with her desire. She reached to kiss him again, but instead he lowered his head down to her breasts. For a moment he kissed them, then he unbuttoned the top of her dress and pushed back the cloth, exposing her full mounds.

"Beautiful," he said simply. "Just beautiful." Canyon reached in and kissed the swell of her right breast, then kissed upward on it to the wide pink areola band and on to the very peak.

"Oh, Lord . . . oh, my," Jill whispered.

He licked her nipple and felt it stiffen and grow.

Jill shuddered. "We better sit down on the bed before I fall over," she said in a small, soft voice.

He let her sit down, then knelt in front of her and bent forward, kissing the other breast, washing off her nipple, and feeling the pulsating heat of both orbs.

A small wail came from Jill. It was a lover's song that slanted around the room without words. She trembled. His hands replaced his lips and he caressed both big breasts at once. Her eyes rolled up and she shivered, then quickly she pushed the dress off her shoulders and pulled it down to her waist. She lifted the chemise over her head and thrust her chest forward, stretching her breasts toward him.

"Lordy, lordy, that feels so wonderful, Canyon. Just so marvelous." She shivered a little.

Canyon murmured and bent to kiss her breasts again. He soon nibbled at her nipples, biting them.

"Oh, God . . . I can't stand that. I can't hold it." She pulled him on the bed, rolled him over, and lay on top of him half on and half off the bed. Her hips pounded at him. She shrilled a wild screech and then a thousand vibrations shook her body once, then twice, then once more before her body quit heaving and pounding and surging with one shattering spasm after another.

Her face twisted into an expression of intense pain and then total pleasure as she fell heavily on top of him.

Canyon felt his manhood surging in its cramped quarters. He was breathing hard himself now as she lifted up and kissed his lips tenderly.

She looked at him in awe. "Nobody ever set me off so quick before," she said. "Let's keep going." She unbuttoned his vest and then his shirt and caressed his chest, twisting his red chest hair around her fingers.

Canyon pulled her forward until he could kiss her breasts.

"Oh, God, I love it when you do that," she moaned.

He pushed one hand down her leg and back up again and she shivered and watched him. He worked his hand up under her skirt to her waist.

A moment later she lifted the dress off over her head and threw it on the floor. "I'm so hot I could explode." She found his belt and then his fly and quickly pulled off his boots, then his pants.

Canyon pushed her down on the bed and she rolled toward him, pushing one smooth, bare leg over his hairy one, drawing it back and forth.

His hands worked down her round little belly, then over her pubic mound and stopped, caressing it, then plunged lower into the dark forest.

His hand stroked her, pressed her, fondled her, and her moans picked up into a chant of love and desire that flooded the room.

Canyon pressed lower, dropped his hand to her soft white inner thighs inches from her moist nest, and she wailed, urging him on.

"Yes, Canyon, find me. Yes, yes, I need you to touch me there. Hurry, Canyon." Jill twisted her hips to put her crotch under his hand. Her breathing was like a steam engine and her knees suddenly spread wide, then snapped closed only to open again slowly, inviting him to come and find her. "Canyon, damn you, touch me!"

His hand found her warm moist entry and stroked it. Jill shrilled in pleasure, a high note of triumph and winning, and then her voice grew low and her hips writhed. Her hand pressed his fingers harder into her until he felt her juices across his whole hand.

She let go of his hand and pulled him over her, urging him forward. Her hands caught at his shaft and guided him. Gently he rested his manhood against her moist, throbbing opening, then eased inward a half-inch.

Jill screamed in delight, thrusting her hips upward, capturing another inch of him, then she caught his tight buttocks with both her hands and drove him forward until their pelvic flesh ground together.

"More of you," she whispered. Then she lifted her knees and her feet and purred like a kitten. She writhed against him, her hips pumping and grinding, saving nothing, letting all of her love pour out and envelop him and entrance him, letting the power of sex win every battle.

They moved together, slowly, rubbing and feeling the hot exciting sensations of flesh against flesh, the internal and the external, sounding out every erotic spot on the human body.

Her hips ground and twisted, her body holding his shaft tightly for its thrustings and withdrawals, and thrusting again as she squeezed him with her thighs and her inner muscles until he moaned at the sensations.

Jill accompanied the sexual dance with her singing, soft and sweet. As their passion built, the song became more frenzied and at last demanding and urgent.

He led her, stroking gently at first, then maintaining the pace and slowly quickening it until he was slamming into her with a growing need and a building intensity that he was sure would kill him. No body could stand this kind of heat, this depth of passion, this exploding need to climax.

Then her whole body seemed to clutch at him and she moaned. The song stopped and she pounded upward to meet his thrusts, her face tightening and twisting as she strained to reach some plateau of existence. Then she exploded, a roar of pain and pleasure and ecstasy billowing from her mouth, cascading around the room as she gave one last thrust upward and then shattered as the last series of powerful spasms shook her until he thought she would surely come apart limb from limb.

Canyon had matched her march to fulfillment, and he roared as his own orgasm exploded in a tremendous intensity that he couldn't control, let alone stop. It blasted his hips forward a dozen more times, plunging through her and up to the pinnacle of physical pleasure before he spasmed and shattered into a myriad of stars to populate the universe.

He sagged and then collapsed over her. They lay there, drained and without moving for several minutes. She held him tightly for another five minutes, then relaxed.

"You all right?" she asked.

"I think I died and went to heaven," Canyon said.

"That good?"

"Yes."

"Best for me, too. Can you stay the rest of the night?"

"I'll try. Not sure what I need to be doing, just yet. But I'll worry about that tomorrow."

He lifted away from her and she gasped as he left her.

"I miss you already," she said, then sat up, her breasts swaying and bouncing delightfully. "I really need you to stay all night," she said suddenly. "I don't get a wonderful man like you in my bed often. I want to keep you for a while. I don't know anything about you. But we've got all night to talk."

She jumped off the bed, hurried into the kitchen, and brought back a whiskey bottle and two small glasses. She poured them each a drink and they sipped at them. They talked and drank, and when the glasses were empty, she put them both away.

"Right now, Canyon O'Grady, I want to see how good you are the second time around. Let's see just how good a lover you really are."

Canyon showed her.

4

The next morning Jill woke Canyon up at five o'clock. "Such a happy big boy," she whispered when she saw he was awake. She held on tightly to his nearly erect phallus and grinned. "Oh, God, but he wants me one more time before I have to get to the café. If I don't open on time, people get angry and start to yell at me."

She settled her naked form over him and eased down flesh to flesh, then dropped a breast into his mouth. Canyon grinned and obliged.

Jill hurried then, seducing him quickly, teasing him just a moment, then she settled over his thighs, her knees spread on each side of his hips. She squealed and lowered herself on him, impaling his shaft into her well-lubricated slit.

"Oh, but that is fine," she yelped. She dropped down on his rock-hard erection until their bones ground together, then she began moving her hips in a small circle, building his passion with each second. She drove into a quick orgasm, panting and screeching in delight and then urging him on. Before Canyon knew what had happened, he exploded with a grunt and then a long low sound that he didn't make often.

When he had found enough strength, he shook his head at her. "So fast! You pushed me too fast."

"Good for you now and then to know who's in charge," Jill said. She pulled away from him and sat up, her big breasts sagging just a little from their bulk. "What a beautiful way to start the day!" Jill stretched and smiled at him. "I wish we had time for one more." She shrugged and then dressed as he watched.

He never failed to appreciate a woman dressing. It was such a ritual. When the last button was fastened and the last snap secured, Jill bent and kissed him.

"You turn over now and have another nap, and when you want to get up, you come inside the café for the best breakfast the place has to offer."

Canyon looked at the windup alarm clock on the dresser. It was five-thirty and getting light. "I better get moving, too. Full day ahead."

A half-hour later Canyon left the livery stables after paying the stable hand a silver dollar to forget that he had been there or that he had left. It might help. He rode out of town behind the livery so no one would see him, curved to the south stage road a mile out, and walked Cormac another two miles before he found a place to wait in a splotch of heavy brush near the river.

The stage road was less than fifty yards away and he could see anyone on the trail. He tied Cormac, lay down in a grassy spot, and took a small nap. If an animal or a horse came within a hundred yards of him, he would be instantly awake with his six-gun in his hand.

Two hours later he awoke. Three horsemen rode down the trail from town to the south. Canyon could tell that the one in the center was Paddy. He rode with his right arm inside his shirt, like in a sling. That round in the side must still be bothering him. Good.

The trio rode on past at a walk, in no rush. The stage wasn't due until four in town; that would make it after three along here.

Canyon mounted up and followed them, moving from one clump of brush and trees to the next, never long in sight, but he saw none of the three check the back trail.

About five miles down the trail they slowed and began, evidently, to pick the spot for the ambush. They found a place where the trail went through a heavily wooded stretch. The rig would have to stay on the road here and they could control it.

The two men with Paddy seemed to be doing most of the deciding. They used ropes and their horses to position downed trees across the road quickly.

A half-hour after they got the trap set up, one of the men rode off to the south, evidently to be an early warning that the stage was coming.

Canyon wasn't sure why they went through with the stopping routine after Paddy knew the sheriff must know about the plan. Maybe it was so near to completion that they couldn't stop it. Maybe they had to do it on the chance the sheriff didn't believe him and the politicians were still on board. Now it was a case of wait and see.

As Canyon watched the pair at the roadblock, he saw another pair of men moving up through the thick brush and trees a quarter of a mile off the stage road. Both men moved cautiously, keeping to the timber whenever possible and working through the high country as if they were stalking someone.

By the time they were five hundred yards away, Canyon could make out a bay and a roan and two men in dark clothes. Each saddle carried a boot and a rifle. They vanished into heavy timber and O'Grady lost them for a while. The next time he spotted them they were about fifty yards away on the other side of the road and on a slight rise, so they had an open view of the roadblock.

They left their horses there and worked slowly forward through light brush to a spot twenty yards closer to the two men who were waiting. Canyon was sure that Paddy and his friend could not see or know of the new arrivals.

Both men had brought their rifles with them and now seemed to be setting up fields of fire and getting ready. They looked like snipers . . . An execution squad?

Now things were getting complicated. Paddy was supposed to stop the stage and probably get everyone out of it. That meant that the governor or the senator could be shot from ambush. The killers would get away with no one even seeing them, and Paddy would be wanted for murder.

What was going on? No one set up a U.S. senator or a territorial governor for murder without some mighty important reason. Canyon wondered what Professor Offenhauser would have to say about this.

Everyone waited another hour. Then, well before Canyon expected it, the rider came charging back from the south. He said something to his cohorts. The three men faded back into the trees on the far side of the road where the riflemen also hid. Now Canyon could see that all three ambushers carried shotguns as well as their six-guns. This could be bad.

Ten minutes later, he heard the team coming and the squeak of an axle and jangle of the harness. The coach came around a small bend in the road. The driver immediately saw the barricade. He must have known it wasn't just a tree blown down across the road because he stopped the rig and quickly tried to turn it around. A shotgun blast over his head halted the try.

Canyon was close enough he could hear it all.

"Stand steady and nobody gets killed," Paddy roared at the stagecoach from hiding.

"Everyone out of the coach, right now," another voice bellowed. This one heavier, with more authority.

"Now," a third voice cracked at them, and a shotgun went off, again firing over the top of the coach.

Slowly a short fat man climbed down from the rig, missing the small metal peg for a step, then making it. Two women came out next and then the driver stepped down.

"Get the others out," Paddy brayed at the people standing near the coach.

"Three fares, all I got today," the driver called.

"Liar," Paddy shouted. He raced out of his hiding spot waving a shotgun. He had a mask over his lower face and rushed to the coach and looked inside. He stepped back and shook his head. "Damn. All right, your purses and wallets and jewelry. Hand it over, right now!

"Where's the strongbox?" Paddy asked the driver.

"Don't got one on this run. Never anything that valuable coming up this way."

Paddy hit him with his six-gun, knocking him down. McNamara jumped up on the rig and looked under the driver's seat, then in the front boot and then the rear, but found no strongbox. He swore to himself and backed slowly into the woods.

Canyon had been watching the men with the rifles. They had waited, their eyes steady at the sights, fingers on triggers. But when the short, fat drummer came out of the stage with a sample case, they looked at each other and shook their heads.

As soon as Paddy made certain there were no more riders in the rig, the two riflemen began to withdraw, moving silently and slowly back the way they had come. Five minutes later, Canyon saw them reach their horses and head back toward town.

On the stage road below, Paddy and his two men had vanished into the thick timber. The driver scratched his head, loaded his people, and then checked the roadblock. It wasn't as thick as it looked. He drove to the end of it and rolled the heavy rig over the small ends of the dead trees, then drove on for Santa Fe.

Canyon ran back to his horse, cut across the road well in front of the coach, and raced after the pair of riflemen. If he could tail them back to some contact in Santa Fe, he might be able to find out who hired them.

He kept a half-mile behind them. The tracking was no problem. The two men had cut back to the stage trail and rode at a canter most of the way back to Santa Fe, not looking behind them. Canyon didn't get close to them. Once they knew they had a tail, they would not go back to the man who hired them.

When they got to the edge of town, Canyon closed the gap to about three hundred feet. He took off the light jacket he had worn, and doffed his hat so he would appear to be someone else if they were checking on a tail.

After three city blocks they came to the downtown area and Canyon had to move up even closer on the men. He spotted them riding down another block, then turning up an alley. He got to the same alley and tied his horse and meandered up the strip, watching the two riders.

About halfway up, they stopped at a building and went in the back door. It was the same building where Archibald Forester had his offices.

But did the men go to see Forester? On the last block of the ride he had been close enough to see that both men were medium-sized. One wore a brown hat and one a black one, but he wasn't sure that he could pick them out of a group of men if he had to. No, he couldn't identify them.

What else was in this building? He walked through a vacant lot to the main street and down to the front of the white building. He saw the signs of three business firms. One was a lawyer, one a surveyor, and one the offices of Archibald Forester, investment counselor.

Without breaking stride, Canyon opened the door and stepped inside. There was a long hallway that must extend to the rear exit. On the side were several doors, some with names on them. He went to the one for

Forester and pushed it open. He entered a small office with a desk, but no one was sitting behind it.

Canyon waited a moment, then left. He checked the other two offices, which were smaller. In each case the proprietor looked up and spoke to him. Canyon asked where he could find the doctor's office and received a courteous answer. There had been no one else in either room. So it was possible that the two men were talking to Forester in a back room. Possible, but not enough to hang a man for.

What he needed was some hard evidence, and right now he didn't have the slightest idea where to get it.

Canyon went down the street to the sheriff's office. He was in.

"It was a bust for Forester. Your word got through on the stagecoach and the dignitaries weren't there."

"Probably a good thing," Sheriff Parrish said. "My man missed the stage. What else happened?"

Canyon told him and the sheriff nodded. "Damn good thing we kept them from getting on that stage. When the one tomorrow morning leaves, there'll be four riflemen and two shotgunners along besides the two politicians. That should make them feel safe enough to travel."

"You heard anything from Washington yet about my getting assigned to this?"

"Not a chance. It's only been two days."

"Seems longer. Until I hear from them officially, I'm just skidding around on an icy boardwalk."

"You're still a sworn peace officer and you have authority here whether they assign you or not. If they don't, I can swear you in as a special deputy."

"Let's hope it doesn't come to that," Canyon said.

He left and went to the café. He was hungry, which reminded him he hadn't had anything to eat since breakfast.

Jill glowed happily when Canyon walked in. He sat at the counter and she brought him a big cup of coffee.

"Get done what you wanted to?" Jill asked, her eyes bright, her chest lifting and falling a little too rapidly.

"Partly," he said. "What's for supper?"

The beef stew was good. He paid and slipped out after he ate without seeing her again. He couldn't afford another night at her place, in spite of the side benefits. He needed to make the rounds of the saloons and gambling halls to see what he could find out about Forester and the territorial governor. They might be in cahoots on some skulduggery. If so, there might be some talk in the saloons about it.

Three hours of working the nickel beer and the dime poker games resulted in his consuming six beers and winning a dollar and twenty cents. However, he learned absolutely nothing about the political situation in the New Mexico territorial capital.

Canyon gave up and went back to his room in the Blue Spruce Hotel. He locked the door, turned the key half a turn, and left it in the lock. Then he pushed the back of a straight chair under the door handle. Anyone coming in would have to make a hell of a racket. O'Grady went to sleep as soon as he dropped on the lumpy mattress.

5

Canyon lay on the bed under one thin sheet to shield him from the crisp night air of the seven-thousand-foot altitude. He rolled over and then sat up, totally awake in an instant. He'd heard something. Footsteps?

Where? He listened again and heard it, soft touches of boot to wood on the outside of the wall. But his room was on the second floor. He heard the soft sound again. He grabbed the mattress on the bed, pulling it with him as he slid off the bed frame to the floor. He landed next to the wall with the mattress shielding him.

Only a second later a shotgun blasted. The first round filled with double-aught buck shattered the window and sprayed deadly .32-sized lead balls across half the room. The second round churned up the other half of the room, but the mattress soaked up the force of the lead rounds with only two of them working through the tightly packed cotton batting.

In the roaring silence after the second shot, Canyon heard the steps going back up the wall toward the roof. The man had lowered himself over the roof on a rope to his window.

Canyon jerked on his boots, grabbed his six-gun belt, and strapped it on as he ran. He raced out the door, down the hotel's back steps and out the door into the alley.

A half-minute later a coil of rope sailed over the roof and dangled in the alley behind the hotel. Next a man appeared and started down. He had a shotgun tied over his back.

Canyon waited until the bushwhacker was halfway down the rope, then he lifted his six-gun and shot at his legs. In the dark it was a hard shot and it took a second round before he hit the man's right leg and knocked him to the ground. He fell and hit the hard packed ground in the alley, shouting in terror.

Canyon stomped on the man's hand when he grabbed for his six-gun.

"You won't be needing that, bushwhacker," Canyon said softly. "No need for firearms in hell." He lifted his own revolver and aimed it at the man's head.

"You just shotgunned my room on the second floor. Who are you and who hired you to do it?"

"God, it hurts. Get me to a doctor."

"What's your name?"

"Dickerson, Alton Dickerson. My leg's broken. Carry me down to the doctor."

"Not until you tell me who hired you to kill me."

"Damn, you're the guy who lives there. Shit . . ."

"Who hired you?"

"Forester, Archibald Forester. He didn't say use the window, I just figured it would be—"

A rifle snarled from less than fifty feet away. Canyon dived behind a big wooden packing crate. Alton Dickerson swore, then he coughed and fell backward to the ground. Three more rounds slammed into the area, one hitting the ambusher, two more into the wooden box.

Canyon pushed his Colt around the side of the packing box and fired five times toward the muzzle flash, but there was nothing in response. He heard some shuffling sounds, as if someone were heading down the alley. Then all was quiet.

Dickerson was not making any sounds.

Five minutes later Canyon edged out from the safety of the packing box to check the man. He was dead, shot three times. Canyon kicked the corpse and swore. He had a witness who said that Forester had hired him to do murder. The law considered that the same as Forester pulling the trigger himself. He could have brought Forester to trial. But not now. A dead witness wasn't much good convincing a jury.

Canyon walked back into the hotel, reloading his six-gun in the dark as he walked.

He woke up the night clerk, told him about his shotgunned room, and demanded a new one. The clerk gave him Room 214 and Canyon transferred his gear from the old room to the new one. Then he lay on the bed fully clothed. He had pushed the dresser against the window. It was tall enough to cover two-thirds of it.

The room's straight-back chair went under the door handle. He had the Colt on the bed beside him and stared at the ceiling. Canyon didn't like being shot at, especially with double-aught buck. He'd seen a man blown almost in half that way. It had not been a pretty sight.

How in hell could he get Forester? Now it was becoming personal. He'd bring this man to ground if he had to do it without any authorization from Washington. He was a sworn peace officer and he did have authority and jurisdiction here.

A half-hour later, he packed everything in his carpetbag, took his Spencer carbine, and walked down the back stairs, down the street to the café. He went to the side and walked to the house behind.

He found Jill still sleeping. Gently he knelt by the bed, found the open top of her nightgown and began to caress her breasts. She moaned softly and turned more toward him. Jill smiled in her sleep. He kissed her lips with a feather touch, undressed, and slid into bed beside her. She never woke up.

One of her arms came around him in her sleep and she pressed against him. Then Canyon slept. He felt safer here than in the damned hotel. He might never sleep in a hotel again.

When Canyon woke up the next morning, it was to an excited shriek of delight from Jill. She sat upright in bed, staring at his naked torso.

"How in the world . . . ?" She grinned. "When did you come into . . . Oh, Lordy, how wonderful. Dammit, we don't have time to do a good one this morning, but you've got to tell me why you came to stay with me."

He told her as she dressed, and her eyes widened with horror. She kissed him and hugged him tight, then stepped back. "I have to go open up. You stay right here and get some rest. I'll be back after the breakfast rush and we can talk about this some more and have a long, slow lovemaking before your breakfast." She bent and patted his crotch, then kissed his lips and hurried out of the room.

Canyon stared at the windup clock on the dresser. It

was nearly six A.M. and the café was due open. He was hungry. He had to talk to the sheriff. And he was mad.

He kicked off from the bed, dressed, then shaved in hot water off the stove. When he was presentable, he went to the café for a quick breakfast over Jill's pleas to stay longer.

A few minutes later, he met Parrish as he strode down the boardwalk to his office. "Found the body behind the hotel yet?" Canyon asked.

"Nope. You kill him?"

"Shot him in the leg. Some gent with a rifle finished the job, so now I'm short one prosecution witness."

"Against Forester?"

"Right. The dead man in question also pumped two rounds of double-aught buck through my second-floor hotel-room window last night. You can check with the room clerk."

Sheriff Parrish looked up, surprised. "This guy you shot was that tall?"

"With a rope from the roof he was. I caught him coming down in back."

When they got to the spot behind the hotel, all they found were a few drips of dried blood. There were shovel marks, which could have meant that whoever moved the body also shoveled up the bloody dirt and took it away as well.

"No body, no murder," the sheriff said.

Canyon set his jaw and said nothing. Covering up a little murder like this must be nothing to Forester. What else was he planning? Was he going to kill the territorial governor or the U.S. senator, or both?

"Easy enough for us to say no murder, Sheriff, but

I'd wager that Alton Dickerson would sing a different tune for us, if he could. Do you recognize the name?''

"Yes. He's been around town for a while. As I remember, he lost his wife about six months ago and went to pieces. Mostly hangs around the saloons grabbing unfinished drinks.''

"Sorry, Sheriff. Guess I didn't need to bother you, after all.''

Canyon walked back toward the café. He went in and got a cup of coffee and kept his hands warm around it as he tried to figure out the conspiracy. Forester was up to something, but what? Getting the two politicians to come to town seemed to be the core of it. Why?

Jill sat down beside him and frowned at his frown. Then she giggled. ''You look so serious, like the whole world is falling down around you and if you just knew how, you would fix it all.''

''I would.''

''Oh.'' She watched him and her broad grin faded. ''Hey, anything I can do to help?''

''Yes, let me stay at your place for a few nights.'' He held up his hand. ''And on most of those nights there will be only a sweet kiss at bedtime.''

She shrugged. ''Sure, we'll do it anyway you want to. Just . . . just don't let it get around. I still have something of a good reputation in town and . . . you know. . . .''

''Right, I understand. I'll be discreet. What do you know about the professor?''

''Offenhauser?''

''The same.''

''He's old, almost never leaves his house anymore. Goes down to the territorial legislature once in a while and talks with them. I'm not even sure he's a professor. Out here we tend to believe what somebody tells us. If Doc Holtzman says he studied medicine for five years in St. Louis, we tend to believe him. Same way with the professor. You met him?''

''Yes. He seemed to be an educated man.''

She squirmed in her chair. ''Maybe so.''

Canyon watched her a minute. ''You don't really think so. You think he's a phony?''

''No, I just don't like him.''

''Why, Jill?''

''He got his hands on me one day. I mean, really grabbed me. I got to wonder if this is a man who was once a dignified, respected university professor.''

''That's a surprise. I figured he was beyond such activity. Evidently I'm not an expert. But he seems to be the expert on local politics. I think it's time I paid him another visit.''

Ten minutes later Canyon knocked on the professor's door and waited a minute. There was no response. He knocked again and this time he heard movement. The old man was probably a bit hard-of-hearing. The door opened and Professor Offenhauser looked up at Canyon in surprise.

Then he smiled. ''Come in, come in dear boy. It's been a while since you were here last. I could use an intelligent conversation.''

They walked into the parlor and sat down in the overstuffed chairs, and the older man smiled.

''Now, young Mr. O'Grady, what can I do for you?''

''Politics. I'm curious why a U.S. senator is coming to town. And one from Iowa at that. What can he possibly want or gain by traveling out this far in his wanderings?''

"I, too, wondered why he was traveling so far afield," the professor said. "However, I can help you a little. The senator was a friend of the New Mexico Territory from the start. Helped us get organized enough to apply for our territorial status. He comes now and again to help us move toward statehood. Of course, he realizes the residency requirement is still well beyond us. But we all try."

"Well, that's worth knowing. I should tell you that the two dignitaries were set to arrive yesterday on the stage, but they didn't come."

The old man held up one hand palm-upward in resignation. "Who knows about politicians? Another baby to kiss, another talk to give, another rich patron to ask for campaign contributions. They tell me it's a never-ending task being a public servant."

"Then you never held elective office, Professor?"

"Oh, my, no. The thought curdles what's left of my blood. Just knowing politicians is hard enough for me." He rubbed his hands together. "Now that we have the business out of the way, do you have time for a game of chess? It's a passion with me. I dearly love to play. Didn't you tell me when we talked before that you play?"

"I play chess badly, I'm afraid, Professor. You'd probably close in six moves. But one of these days I'll brighten your afternoon with a game or two. I say brighten because I've never seen a man yet who wasn't happier after he beat another at chess."

The professor laughed. "Yes, yes. I remember a man in Boston who told me he played 'a bit' of chess. We had one game and I quickly learned that he was only about two steps away from being a grand master. I brightened several of his days, I assure you."

Canyon stood. "Professor, I won't take up any more of your time, just wanted the expert's opinion about the senator. Now I'll be on my way. Maybe in the next three or four days we can have that chess game."

"Good, good. My hip, would you mind my not walking to the door?"

"You stay right there, Professor. I know the way. When I get some problems cleared up, we'll have that game."

Canyon said good-bye and went out the front door. As he walked away, he soon realized the professor had told him absolutely nothing that wasn't obvious. But that may be because that's all the professor knew about the senator, or cared about him and his friend the territorial governor.

Canyon headed to the newspaper office and went inside. As with most newspapers, there was a rack holding back issues for six months. He began browsing through them, at last concentrating on reading at least part of every story on the front page. The weekly paper grew larger as the months passed.

Soon he knew a lot about Santa Fe, but not much about the territorial government or the governor. Now and then he saw Archibald Forester's name mentioned.

When he looked at the Seth Thomas clock ticking on the wall, he realized it was almost time. He put the papers away and hurried toward the stagecoach station. The governor and U.S. Senator Clark Jamison should be arriving at any minute now.

6

When Canyon O'Grady arrived at the stage depot, the coach hadn't arrived yet. The clerk from inside was standing on the boardwalk looking down the street to the south.

Five minutes later Canyon heard dogs barking and he saw a cloud of dust.

"There she comes, right on time," the clerk shouted. "She'll be here in a minute, folks. Step back and give the horses room to pull in."

Twenty men, women, and small boys waited for the stage. The arrival of the stage was the highlight of the day. No trains came to Santa Fe yet. A half-block down the street, Canyon could see four boys chasing along beside the stage, racing it, and losing as the driver slammed the big rig through the narrow street, yelling at drivers of buggies and wagons to get out of the way.

Every stage driver ever to hold the twelve reins in his hands loved to charge into and out of town. The rest of the ride was much calmer, but tradition dictated a slashing, charging entry and exit.

The big Concord coach came to a stop and the clerk stepped up and opened the door. The first man out was medium-sized, about fifty years old, bespectacled, and nearly bald. He was chunky, with fat, slightly red cheeks, and he was wearing a dark-blue suit and vest and white shirt. As he stepped down, he waved at the crowd.

"United States Senator Clark Jamison from the great state of Iowa at your service, Santa Fe," he said.

The crowd cheered.

Right behind him came a tall and thin man in a gray suit and vest, a homburg hat perched on his head. His face was thin and drawn and slightly sallow-looking. Canyon wondered if he'd been ill. He smiled and waved but didn't announce himself. The senator looked at him.

"My friends, you know your own territorial governor, the honorable Bernard Taggart."

Now the people cheered and waved, and Taggart waved back at them. Then the armed guards came out of the coach and formed a box around the two men and they moved off down the street.

Canyon let out a held-in breath. Both men had arrived safely, and nobody had tried to gun them down when they stepped off the stage. So far, so good. He followed along behind the guards for a ways, letting them get farther ahead. They soon came to a respectably sized house with a well-tended yard. A sign outside announced it was the governor's official residence. The box of guards ushered both men inside.

"That's what I call adequate security," a voice said from behind Canyon. He turned and saw Sheriff Parrish.

"Looks good enough to me," Canyon said. "At least they arrived in one piece and both are still breathing."

"Good, now come and meet them. I'll tell them you're on temporary service with me. The governor likes to know the lawmen in town."

Canyon nodded and fell into step beside Parrish. One of the guards on the door was the sheriff's deputy. A moment later O'Grady and Parrish were inside, hats in hand.

The sheriff did the honors, introducing Canyon to the two politicians, who were hoisting some wine in the governor's private study.

"Well, a fine Irish lad, I'd say," the senator rumbled. His handshake was easy and practiced.

"O'Grady, haven't I heard of you?" the governor asked.

"Probably not, Governor. I spend most of my time out on the road and just recently arrived in town."

"Well, good to have you on board."

Canyon shook the governor's hand. The clasp was warm and honest, but the man still looked ill. There was a flurry at the side of the room and Canyon heard a high, lilting laughter.

A girl swept into the room in a showy dress that left the tops of her breasts in glorious exhibition. She smiled at the men, nodded at the governor, and stopped in front of Canyon. Her gaze was unmistakable.

Senator Jamison stepped up quickly.

"Mr. O'Grady, may I present my daughter, Elyse. Elyse, this is Canyon O'Grady, who is working with Sheriff Parrish."

She held out her hand to be kissed, and he kissed it gently. Then she held on to his fingers. "Delighted to meet you, Mr. O'Grady. Is it true what I hear about Irish men?''

"That depends, Miss Jamison, on what you have heard," Canyon answered carefully.

"I've heard that they are absolutely fantastic . . ." Elyse looked at her father and grinned. "Fantastic husbands, is that true?" She put her arm through his and walked him away from the politicians.

"Husbands?" Canyon said softly when they were at a safe distance. "I'd wager a twenty-dollar gold piece that isn't what you really intended to say."

They stopped near the heavy drapes of the window well away from the other men in the room. She pulled his arm closer to her until it pressed against her side and the swell of her breast. Then she looked up at him.

"What I would have said was that Irishmen make fantastic lovers. I'm staying at the Blue Spruce Hotel. I got moved out of here since there isn't room for all of Daddy's security people. Room two-thirty-six.

"The reception here will be over by ten-thirty. Daddy is a widower, so I'm his hostess for all of his society things. By eleven I'll have been escorted to my room in the hotel. The guard doesn't stay."

"You can count on eleven o'clock," Canyon said.

She nodded and released his arm and walked back to her father's small group.

Canyon began to move around, talking to some of the guards, watching the political animals in their native habitat. Curiously he liked both of the men. The senator was a blowhard, probably a double-dealer and a conniver, but most politicians were.

Taggart, on the other hand, seemed to be one of the people who was thrust into leadership. He had been appointed by the president, and so he wouldn't be a local. He may have been a territorial governor somewhere else. It was a career job in Washington these days, with five administrators needed for each new territory.

O'Grady walked around the big room, which quickly began to fill with guests. Soon there were at least thirty men milling around, talking. By their conversations, most were politicians, but a few business leaders were also present. Archibald Forester, resplendent in a cutaway jacket and white tie, was one of the most popular men there. He talked with the governor and the senator, introducing them to various other local men, assuming the role of civic leader. Canyon avoided them.

It was nearly five when Canyon talked briefly with the sheriff and excused himself. There was nothing more he could do there and it seemed a wasted effort. In fact, everything he was doing suddenly seemed wasted time and energy. He should be getting to a telegraph office, where he could wire Washington of his conclusion of the last job.

The telegraph lines had advanced well beyond Denver now and were heading for Utah. But he was a long way from Denver. Up the Santa Fe Trail the first real town would be Independence, Missouri. It probably had a telegraph office by now, but he was eight hundred miles from there.

Canyon marched down the street, frustrated at his inability to find any solid evidence against Forester. When he had left the gathering, he had seen others leaving. The informal session was about over and the formal reception would begin at six-thirty. Canyon had not been invited and was pleased about that.

He walked back to the café, and when Jill motioned to him, he walked back to the counter and sat down.

She put a cup of coffee in front of him.

"You don't look too chipper," Jill said.

"I'm furious because I know something is going on here that I can't stop. I know Forester is as crooked as hell and I don't have a bit of evidence I can use in court. He's tried to kill me at least twice and I can't prove it. He's planning something foul and illegal and I don't have a hint of what it is."

"Go right up to him and accuse him of something," Jill suggested.

"He's a popular man, a leader in the territorial senate; he has a lot of friends. I'd be laughed out of town."

"So wait and watch him," Jill said.

"I've been doing that for three days and it hasn't helped. Besides that, people keep shooting at me. I don't like that. A person could get seriously injured that way."

"What you need is a good meal. People always feel better with something on their stomach." Jill grinned and hurried away. When she came back, she had two slices of bread still steaming, a pot of butter, a jar of jam, and a table knife.

"Enjoy this to start. I've got to finish the roast."

The freshly made butter melted on the warm bread, and for a moment Canyon was back in Brooklyn in his mother's kitchen. Smelling the delicious fragrance of baking bread always had been one of his true joys.

As he worked on the bread and butter and strawberry jam, he decided he could give this project two more days. If nothing happened, he'd have to push on

59

toward a telegraph line where he could get in contact with Washington.

The supper was good, and he kissed Jill on the cheek and told her he had to watch the governor's house tonight. He might be gone all night and told her not to wait up.

He did walk past the governor's mansion. The reception seemed to be going well, and the dinner would follow. He saw three deputy sheriffs patrolling the grounds. Things looked under control.

So, he had to wait. Canyon O'Grady was an action man; waiting around galled him like poison. He settled at last for a quarter-limit poker game at the Red Tailed Saloon and soon found that he was a ten-dollar loser. He buckled down, got some fresh chips, and in three hours had won nearly twenty dollars. The three other players folded and went home for the night.

He had had a beer or two as he played, and when it was ten o'clock, he decided he needed a brisk walk to clear his head before he called on Elyse Jamison at her hotel room.

He did a mile out and a mile back and felt like his old self again. His Waterbury pocket watch showed that it was 10:45 when he climbed the stairs to the second floor of the Blue Spruce Hotel and found Room 236. Canyon hesitated before he knocked.

He snorted at his lack of confidence, knocked, and a moment later the door came open. Elyse stood there, wearing the same dress she had had on that afternoon, only now there was a heavy sweater covering her breasts and up tightly to her neck and down to her wrists.

"Yes, Mr. O'Grady." She stood there watching him.

"May I come in, or would you rather I went away?" Canyon asked.

"No, no, please, come in." She stood to one side and Canyon entered and closed the door. She stood in the middle of the room, watching him.

"Elyse, is something the matter?"

"No, I got chilly, that's all."

"Then you are glad to see me?"

"Of course, Canyon O'Grady. Why wouldn't I be?"

"Maybe because you said more than you meant to this afternoon and now you wished you hadn't said it and now you wish that I'd go home and not bother you."

"No!" She said it loudly and took a step toward him. "I mean, don't go, I'm glad you came."

"You don't seem as enthusiastic about it as you did this afternoon."

"That was my public personality. I do it well. I act as a socializer for my father and am his hostess."

"But when you're out of the spotlight all of that great feeling and confidence just kind of fades away, right?"

She nodded.

"Elyse, why don't you sit down on the bed? I'll sit on the chair and we can talk. I won't touch you. Would that make you feel better?"

"Oh, yes." She sat down. "I know this is silly, but I . . . I don't know how to stop it. I did have a gentleman friend in Washington. He was nice, but then he moved away."

"What shall we talk about?" Canyon asked.

"Oh, I'd love to talk about you. Tell me all about yourself, where you were born, who your parents are, where you went to school, and where you lived, just everything."

"Not much to tell."

"But I want you to. That will help me relax."

Canyon grinned, and so he told her. He spoke of his birth in Ireland, his father's political persecution, how his mother had named him for the dream of America.

"Canyon O'Grady," Elyse said softly. "Yes, I like it, it fits you. What happened when you came to this land?"

"My father went to work with the railroad gangs that built the rail lines all through the East. We lived in Brooklyn for a while, and it was a tough neighborhood. But the more I learned and the more I saw how hard my father had to work, the more I was sure that I wanted a life with some adventure in it. So I moved west into the new frontier, the new way of living."

"Well, now, I do feel better. I like to know something about the people I talk to. I know I should have brought some refreshments from the reception, but I wasn't sure I'd even be able to open the door for you."

"Now, Elyse, tell me something about yourself. Have you always lived in Washington?"

"Oh, no. I grew up in Iowa. Father was a lawyer there and in the state legislature before he was elected to the Senate. That's when we moved to the capital. It's been exciting there. Mother died the second year of father's first term.

"He's in the first year of his second term now, so we have at least five more years in the center of everything. I dreamed of being a teacher, but it's too late for that. Now all I can do is help Father.''

She stood up and walked slowly over to Canyon. In a sudden move she sat down in his lap and reached for his face with hers.

''Canyon O'Grady, I want you to kiss me right now before I lose my nerve.''

7

For just a moment Canyon stared into Elyse's eyes to see if she was sure, and he saw the desire, the pent-up emotion there that told him everything. Mostly it told him to be careful.

He kissed her waiting lips and saw her eyes close well before he touched her. It was a soft, gentle kiss that held little passion and only a hint of a promise.

He came away and her eyes stayed shut. She breathed deeply and then smiled.

Slowly her eyes opened and she sighed. "Oh, my!" She looked at him. "That was so . . . so nice. So soft and gentle. And tender." She watched him closely. "I guess you've been with a lot of girls."

"A few, yes."

"Oh, my." A small frown touched her face. "Would you . . . Mr. O'Grady, would you be so kind as to kiss me again?"

"It would be my pleasure, Miss Jamison."

She closed her eyes and he kissed her, this time with more pressure and more authority, bending her head back a little and bringing her body closer to his so her breasts just touched his chest. He held the kiss longer and a tear slipped out of her eye and down her cheek.

He came away and again her eyes stayed closed.

"Oh, yes, I'm sure now, Mr. O'Grady. That's the most beautiful kiss I've ever had."

My God, I was right: she really is a virgin, Canyon thought.

"I'd guess that you haven't been kissed a lot, Miss Jamison."

"Not a lot. Sometimes at Father's receptions and dinners, a man will steal a kiss behind a screen or in the cloakroom. But not a lot."

This time she didn't ask; she just leaned toward him until her breasts pushed against his chest, and reached her lips up to be kissed. He made the kiss so feathery soft that their lips barely met. He could feel the heat of her breasts through his shirt.

He let the kiss linger, then pressed harder and at last eased up and opened his lips. He swept his tongue once across the length of her soft red lips.

Her eyes popped open in surprise.

"Oh! Oh, my. Yes, I think I like that. Do it again."

He kissed her, and when his tongue touched her lips, they parted. She gasped but didn't retreat. He let his tongue explore in her mouth a moment, then broke off.

"Oh, my goodness! I'm undone. I mean, that is so exciting. I know I shouldn't be saying that, you in my hotel room and all."

He kissed her again and this time her mouth was open and her tongue explored. As it did, his hand slid between them and caught one of her full breasts and he caressed it gently, rubbing it tenderly, brushing her nipple once.

This time there was no gasp, only a straight look. He left his hand on her breast.

"Yes. I like you touching me there." She looked at him with such honest, open, trusting eyes that he nearly ran out the door. "I like it, Canyon. I know I shouldn't, but I do." She caught his hand and pushed it under the sweater and up to the bare tops of her breasts. "It's all right. Now kiss me again."

Instead, he lifted her off his lap and they went to the bed and sat closely together. She pushed his hand under her sweater again and his hand found her warm flesh and pressed under the top of the dress around a breast.

This time she kissed him. Her mouth was open and she the aggressor. She moaned softly as his hand fondled her bare breast, teasing her nipple, then rolling it between thumb and finger.

She shuddered. When the kiss ended, he brought his hand down and caught the sweater and lifted it. When it came to her eyes, she nodded and he took it off over her head, disheveling her short blond hair. She pulled her arms from the sweater and dropped it on the floor. Slowly she lay back on the bed.

He bent over her, kissing first her mouth then her eyes, then her nose and her mouth again. His hand found the bare top of her other breast and he pushed under the dress.

Slowly she unbuttoned four fasteners down the front of her dress and pushed back the material. Her breasts nearly popped out from their confinement.

"Please, Canyon. Kiss them for me. No man has ever kissed them before. I want it to be you."

He touched them with both hands, fondled them, petted them, caressed them, until she was panting.

Then he bent down and kissed both her nipples. Twice he kissed them, then bit on the growing nipples.

Elyse gasped and moaned. He kept kissing her breasts, rubbing them, and then, as she tapered off, he stopped and pulled up her dress to cover her.

Afterward he saw a spot of sweat on her forehead and two tears roll down her cheeks. She sighed again and sat up, her face showing the most beautiful smile he had ever seen.

"Just fantastic," she said softly. "The most wonderful experience of my life. I thank you, Canyon. I think that's all I can ask of you tonight. I know you're probably wishing for more, but I'm so excited I can't even think."

She sat up and held her dress over her breasts. "You're the sweetest, kindest man I've ever known. If I was smart, I'd trick you into marrying me."

He kissed her cheek. "Elyse, you're a beautiful lady. I've never seen such a tiny waist. And your breasts are perfect, a graceful beauty. And I agree. I think it's time that I let you get your beauty sleep."

"One more kiss?"

She held out her arms and pushed her breasts hard against his chest as they kissed, tenderly, then with more passion, and when he came away from her, the top of her dress dropped and she didn't notice it. Her mouth was open and her eyes half-closed as she watched him.

"Again, Canyon. You have to promise to come again. My door will always be open to you at eleven o'clock, I promise."

Canyon stood slowly, reached down, and fondled her breasts once more, then winked at her and slipped out the door. He heard her lock it behind him. What a strange outcome! He had expected a wildcat, already naked and panting and waiting for him. He expected to have scratches all over his back from her fingernails.

Instead, he found a frightened young woman of no experience who wanted everything. Maybe after three or four times in her room they would at last make love. Maybe.

He checked on Room 214 and found that his key still fit. The bed was made and no one else was using it. He slipped in, locked the door, and braced it with a chair. Canyon was asleep almost before he hit the bed.

When he woke, it was daylight. He checked his watch and saw that it was nearly eight o'clock. He pulled on his pants, shirt, and vest, combed his red hair, and hurried down to the café. He went to the back and found his shaving gear and shaved in Jill's bedroom, then went into the café.

She brought him a cup of coffee.

"You heard?" she asked.

"Heard what?"

"Governor Taggart died last night in a buggy wreck out near the two-mile turn. Sheriff is going out about nine o'clock to check on it."

"How did it happen?"

"Nobody seems to know. A traveling man came up the south trail this morning and reported the buggy over the cliff. He recognized the governor and brought back a wallet from his pocket with identification in it."

Canyon ate a fast breakfast, got Cormac from the stable, and met the six men at the sheriff's office a little before nine. He looked around. The senator wasn't there. Neither was Archibald Forester.

Sheriff Parrish looked up and waved. "Hoping you would hear and come along," he said. "The senator claims he can't ride, bad back and a bad hip. Forester hasn't been on a riding horse in ten years. We're ready."

Trailing a spare horse to bring back the body they rode out.

"Any idea how it happened?" Canyon had settled in to ride beside the lawman.

"None. Most of the folks in town knew that the governor loved to drive a buggy. He liked to go fast and he used to challenge all comers in buggy races. Now and then he liked to take out a buggy for a run. My guess is he went out last night to kind of unwind after the big reception and got into trouble on that curve."

"Then he knew the roads around here like his back yard," Canyon said.

"Yep."

"Damn convenient. It could be that the governor was the target all along. Since the two riflemen missed him at the roadblock, they waited until he went driving and did the job then."

"Possible, but I don't want you spreading that idea around. Let's look and see what we find, and then evaluate it. If he don't have a bullet in him, your theory won't hold up."

"It works even better without a bullet. If I was doing the job, I'd be damn sure to make it look like an accident, wouldn't you? No bullet holes. A gun butt against the head perhaps, then scare the horse, aim him off the side of a drop-off . . ."

"Don't spread that around either. All we can do is find the facts and report them to the legislature. That's our job."

"Might be yours, but I'm not bound by any chain of command here, Sheriff. I don't work for you."

"I remember. The senator figured that out last night at the reception. But I didn't tell him who you really are. Hell, let's just play it smart here until we find out what we're dealing with."

"I can tell you that, Sheriff. Without even looking at the evidence, I can guarantee that this is a murder."

It was only two miles to the curve where the stage road began to climb up the side of a ridge. At that point the road had to cross before it came to the pass and then the ride down to Albuquerque.

On a horse it wasn't so impressive, and Canyon hardly remembered it. But in a buggy or a stagecoach it would be quite a grade.

The sheriff saw the spot where the rig went over the side and he stopped everyone fifty yards from it. He sent two men down the slope to check on the condition of the governor. He and Canyon walked their horses up the road, ground-tied them well back of the tracks, and walked up and checked. On the road twenty yards from where the buggy crashed over the drop-off, Canyon found what he was hunting for. He discovered a single set of hoofprints beside another set of hoofprints. The ones on the outside had been partly covered up by the wheels of the buggy.

A rider could have held the buggy horse's head and led it to the edge of the road.

He looked directly behind the buggy and found three sets of fresh hoofprints that had been made over the buggy wheel tracks. Three men could have followed and frightened the buggy horse with whoops and shouts and gunshots.

Canyon showed the tracks to Sheriff Parrish and explained what they could mean. The sheriff only nodded grimly.

They followed the tracks of the buggy to the very edge, saw where the horse and rig must have hit and gouged out the dirt on the cliff face maybe fifty feet down. Then it had rolled and smashed and crashed another hundred feet to the bottom of the small draw.

The horse had broken free of the smashed buggy and lay to one side, its head crushed.

A man came up and shook his head at the lawman.

"Sheriff, he's gone. Looks like he's been dead eight or nine hours at least. Getting stiff before long."

"Thanks, Doc. Get that spare horse down here and tie him however you can. Guess we should have brought a wagon for him."

"Doctor Holtzman, did you find any wounds on the body?" Canyon asked.

"Wounds? No bullet marks. I checked pretty good. None on the heart or head that would kill him. Half his bones are broken and the back of his head is smashed up pretty bad. Face isn't touched. Big gash on his chest from a rock or part of the buggy."

Canyon nodded. "His head, Doctor. Did it look like the result of the fall and rolling and hitting the rocks? Or could the governor have been dead before he went over the drop-off?"

"Well, yes and no. His head is smashed up bad. But

how can we say it didn't happen on the way down? On the other hand, there's a lot of damage. A club could have done it. No way to tell exactly when the man died, before or after the fall.''

"Doctor, I'd appreciate it if you keep our conversation private. It's important.''

"Sure, no problem for me since you're working with the sheriff.''

Parrish had been standing there waving some of the other men away as the three of them talked. Now he directed the men tying the governor on the horse.

"We'll stop outside of town and send somebody in for a wagon,'' Sheriff Parrish said. "No way for a governor to be brought into his capital.''

It took them a half-hour to get the horse loaded and the body moved up the slope to the road. Then it was another half-hour to ride the two miles back to town.

The sheriff said nothing to Canyon on the way back. Canyon had decided that the governor had been clubbed to death, then the buggy driven out here and the horse forced over the cliff with the governor inside the rig.

After a fall like that, murder would be hard to prove. He couldn't use the body to prove murder, so he had to find the killers. Right now he was concentrating on the two men he had seen going into Forester's office and Paddy McNamara. Where had the little man vanished to?

Canyon rode up beside the doctor and chatted awhile. Then he got to the point.

"Doc, I met a guy named Paddy McNamara the other day. He had been shot on his side. How's he doing?''

"Came in twice to see me. His side is healing. Came out of it lucky if you ask me. As I remember, you're the one who shot him."

"Right, we used to know each other when we were ten years old back in Brooklyn in New York."

"Small world sometimes, isn't it?" Dr. Holtzman said. "Paddy should be checking back in once more today or tomorrow."

Canyon nodded and rode away.

8

Halfway to town from the crash site, Canyon peeled off and rode back the way they had come. "I need to take another look at the crash and the buggy," Canyon told Sheriff Parrish. There were a lot of questions he didn't have answers for.

They had met the morning stage heading for Albuquerque, so any tracks that might have helped on the roadway were obliterated by the team of six and the four big wide coach wheels.

He rode into the canyon and up to where the horse lay. The animal's legs were broken and it had hit hard on its head. Its back might be broken too. He checked all of the animal he could see, but could find nothing suspicious.

Canyon tied a rope from his saddle on the front two feet of the buggy horse and looped it around his saddle horn and turned the dead horse over on its other side. It was stiff already.

He examined the other side of the dead animal. He was about to give up when he found what he hunted for. The inch-wide wound on the side of the horse's head where a slug, probably a rifle round, had come out. It had made such a small puckered hole on the entry side that he didn't even see it through the dark hair.

The animal must have been forced to walk up to the very edge of the bank, but then couldn't be frightened to take another step. So she had been shot and had fallen forward over the brink, pulling the buggy with the already beaten-to-death governor in the seat. So they both were dead before they went over the cliff.

Neatly done, but in the dark they didn't think to check the horse. They should have used a rock and smashed and torn the exit wound so it couldn't be identified as such.

Canyon looked over the rest of the buggy wreckage. There was blood on the seat. There was a great deal of blood, seemingly much more than should be there, for the governor had been thrown out of the rig before it hit the bottom and rolled and fell part of the way.

The U.S. agent could find nothing else. No obvious gunshot holes in the torn canvas top of the rig. No splintered holes where bullets could have hit the sides or the wheels.

But now he had enough. Even without any conclusive proof from the body, he was convinced that it was murder. Proving it would be another matter without a confession.

Who? Paddy and the two thugs? Possible. Paddy was the one he knew. He'd ride back to town and find a hidden spot where he could watch the doctor's office without being seen.

First he reported to the sheriff what he had found. The sheriff sighed and looked out the window. "I don't need a murder like this one right now, O'Grady. Fact is, it could have been the rider who came in this morning who found the horse busted up and put her out of her misery.''

"Not a chance. The carcass was stiff as a two-by-four. She'd been dead at least twelve hours by the time I rolled her over. I'm betting it happened about the way I laid it out. Nothing else answers all of the questions. How about the blood on the buggy seat? If he got thrown out and killed on the way down, there wouldn't be any blood at all on that seat.''

"I see what you mean. But like you say, suspicions are one thing, proving them something else again. I'll keep a file on it. Write up what you told me for the file and we'll watch it closely.''

"That's all you're going to do?''

"What else can I do? Who do you suggest I arrest?''

Canyon glowered. "Dammit, that's the problem dealing with a really smart killer. He covers all of his tracks. But we'll find him.''

"You hear the lieutenant governor called a special meeting of both houses of the legislature? Having a memorial service for Taggart and then the betting is the politicians will suggest a successor. Won't be a sure thing, though. The territorial governor is always appointed by the president.''

"Yeah, we'll see what happens. I got me some business.'' Canyon walked out of the sheriff's office unhappy that the lawman wasn't more aggressive. But he did see his point: there wasn't much either of them could do right now to resolve the matter. Evidence, they needed evidence they could take into court.

Canyon found the doctor's office and walked in. The doctor spoke before Canyon was across the threshold.

"In answer to your question, I did do a quick autopsy on Taggart. I found no other cause of death except the extreme trauma to the head. Curiously enough, however, I did find bits and pieces of splinters embedded in the skull. I'm no expert, but they seem to be from some sawn piece of lumber such as a two-by-four and not from any of the wood used on the buggy frame or roof braces.''

''Now we're getting somewhere.'' Canyon heard excitement creeping into his voice. ''The governor was beaten to death with a two-by-four. Doctor, could I ask you to keep this report confidential for a few days? Misplace it on your desk or something. Don't even give it to the sheriff. Looks like we've got a hell of a big conspiracy here, and I don't know who I can trust. I will trust you this much.''

He took out his identification card from the president and showed it to the doctor.

''Well, now,'' Dr. Holtzman said after he had read it. ''Working directly for President Buchanan, huh? Be damned.''

''Understand I'm not on assignment here, just stopped by, but ran into something that smells extremely bad. So I'm asking your confidence on this. Oh, one more thing: there was a lot of blood on that buggy seat. Head wounds bleed a lot, don't they?''

''Blood all over the place.''

''If the governor was beaten while he sat on the buggy seat, he'd bleed a lot right there, correct?''

''Yes.''

''But if he was thrown out of the buggy and smashed his head into the rocks as he fell, there wouldn't be a drop of blood on that smashed-up buggy seat, would there?''

77

"True, Canyon. And once the heart stops pumping, a wound stops bleeding. Like stopping pumping water from a well."

"Thanks, Doctor Holtzman. And remember, don't say a word of any of this to anyone. Stall them on the autopsy if you have to. Oh, has Paddy stopped by yet?"

"He left me a note last night. Said he was hurting and he'd be in this morning, but so far I haven't seen him."

"Thanks, don't mention that you saw me. It could be important as well."

Canyon looked up and down the street, then slipped out quickly and crossed to the edge of the alley. He pulled a wooden packing crate down the alley ten feet and arranged it so he had a perfect view of the doctor's office while staying hidden.

Then he settled down to wait.

Noon came and passed and still Paddy had not shown up. It was after one o'clock before Canyon spotted his long-ago friend coming down the street. He was holding his left arm against his side and taking short, controlled steps. The man was hurting.

Should he go in now and take Paddy and make him talk, or wait and follow him, hoping he would lead to the other two men he figured Forester had hired? He knew he had to wait.

A half-hour later, Paddy came out the doctor's front door. He paused a moment, then turned back the way he had come and walked slowly down the street. Canyon followed him well back. Twice Paddy looked behind him. Once Canyon could step into an alley. The other time he stared into a saddlemaker's window as he scratched the side of his head to hide his face.

Both times Paddy kept going. He turned down the next side street, walked a full block, and went up the path to a white two-story house. He went in without knocking.

Canyon watched the house for ten minutes, then walked close enough to read the sign near the door. He kept his hat well down over his face. The sign read: ANDERSON'S BOARDING HOUSE.

Canyon turned around and went back to the café. At least he knew where Paddy had settled in. Now, what? Visit him tonight? Wait until he came out and grab him? Or tail him and see where he went next?

He walked slowly, thinking it through. He had missed something. The killing, the hoofprints in the roadway. Suddenly he snapped his fingers and took off at a run for the livery stable. He had remembered what he should have done when he was out at the crash site. He saddled Cormac and rode out of the livery by the back door. When he was out of sight of the last of the town buildings, he turned south and pushed the palomino to a canter to eat up the miles.

When he came at the point on the stage road where the buggy had gone over the side, he studied it carefully. How would he do it? His guess was that they had caught the governor on a nighttime outing at the edge of town and forced him to drive up here. He was killed here with a club, the horse shot, and the rig pushed over the edge.

Then, what?

That was the whole point. The two or three riders had to leave, had to ride back to town or somewhere else. Where did they go? They had to leave this very spot. How would they do it? He looked around. They wouldn't go down the cliff, for damn sure. The other side of the road sloped up gently, easy enough to ride along and still stay off the road and not leave any more prints in the thick road dust.

O'Grady rode two hundred yards down the road to-ward town, ground-tied Cormac at the edge, and be-gan to make a close examination of the ground. He worked a semicircle that would swing around the spot where the buggy went over. Somewhere on that half-circle he should find a trail of one or more horses leaving the scene. He had an idea they did not walk away, but put their mounts into a gallop for the first quarter of a mile.

He bent over and stared at the ground as he walked in the half-circle. He was less than a quarter of the way around when he found one set of new hoof prints. Twenty yards farther on, he found two more sets of hoof prints: the mounts had been running fast, throw-ing up little scuffs of dirt with the front of the hoof.

He turned and followed the prints back to the road-way. He found where the horses had been tied for some time. He looked at the sun and ran for his horse. It was getting on toward four o'clock. Why hadn't he thought of this idea this morning? Now he had maybe three hours of daylight left.

He mounted and worked back to the three sets of hoof prints and followed them. They moved north, paralleling the stage road to town.

Another quarter of a mile and the three set of prints turned to the east. Canyon stopped and looked at the long view. He knew the town was ringed with mountains. Those to the east were the Sangre de Cristo Range. But their high peaks were a long way off.

As he rode following the tracks cross-country, he soon found that they led along a small stream that worked up a long valley toward some foothills. Soon the tracks came close to a blush of growth along the stream and he had cover as he worked to the east and now north again. The three sets of tracks showed that the horses had slowed and here they had plodded along, as if the riders knew where they were going.

Canyon pushed through the brush and then across the hock-deep little creek to survey the other side of the valley. He could see no habitation, and no smoke from a fire.

An hour later the sun was starting to flirt with the mountains far to the west. This time when he moved through the brush, he spotted smoke another half-mile upstream.

As it worked higher, the small creek had less and less water and the brush thinned until he felt it was unsafe to move any farther until dusk. He stopped in a heavy spot of brush and let Cormac have a long drink, chomp on some late shoots of green grass by the creek.

Now he could smell the smoke. They must not be afraid of showing where they were. How could they be so careless? If they did kill the governor, they should have posted a lookout at least this far from the cabin. Perhaps they had and he hadn't spotted the visitor yet.

With dusk and his newfound concealment, Canyon left the horse where he was and worked upstream on foot, carrying the Spencer. He went through the brush like an Apache, not breaking a twig or letting a branch swish back.

When he figured he was close to the cabin, he crawled through the light brush on the far side of the tiny stream and parted some high grass to check on the place.

It had the looks of an old miner's cabin, maybe twelve feet square, made of logs with a wooden roof that had been sodded over. A good freeze and they'd have a leak-proof ceiling.

A light glowed in the single window. He could see the outline of a door, and a minute later somebody opened the door and threw out some water.

When the door closed, Canyon looked around the small cleared space by the cabin but couldn't see anything. Nothing moved. He watched for the glow of a cigarette of a man bored with his guard duty, but couldn't even find that. There might be no outside watchman.

Back on the far side of the chattering little stream, he moved silently up until he was directly across from the cabin. Now he could hear someone talking inside, or singing. The lilt of a harmonica came through the air, and he nodded.

The sound would be plenty of cover for him to get to the window. He went across the inch-deep water and darted to the side of the cabin, the rifle in one hand, his cocked six-gun in the other.

He crouched at the wall and got his breath back. No one had shown outside. They were all in the cabin. He took off his hat, lifted up, and looked over the bottom of the lowest windowpane.

Inside, in faint light of two kerosene lamps, he saw

three men. None of them was Paddy McNamara. Canyon breathed a sigh of relief. He wouldn't have to face that just yet, at least. He studied the layout. The door went in from his left. It was one big room with a table and stove to the right. Bunks along the wall would hold six men. He saw blankets in three of them.

Two of the men still wore their gun belts. One sat at the table, the other stood nearby. The third, at the stove, evidently was the cook and had his gun leather hanging over the back of a straight chair. The furniture was handmade from timber, and heavy. On a shelf to the side of the stove he saw enough food to last the trio for a week.

Now he wished he had the scattergun. Almost nobody would draw against a sawed-off shotgun. It couldn't take out all three of them with one shot, but it could kill two in one blast.

He lifted the Spencer carbine, braced the stock against his arm, and held it with his left hand, finger on the trigger. Yes, it would do for one shot.

Canyon wished he could tell if the door had a bolt on it. Chances are that if it did, it wouldn't be thrown this time of day. He crept over to the door and made sure the six-gun was cocked and there was a round in the Spencer's chamber.

A second later he kicked the door open, surged inside with the two weapons covering the two men with guns.

"Move and you're dead," Canyon bellowed.

The man at the stove spun and dived for his weapon six feet away. Canyon swung the six-gun his way and blew a hole through his head before he hit the rough plank floor.

As the one man came uncovered, he flashed his hand to his hip and produced a revolver. He got off a shot before Canyon could swing the heavy carbine to cover him and fire.

The rounds went off almost at the same time. Canyon saw his round lance into the gunman's side and spin him backward just as something hit Canyon in the thigh and slammed him against the wall. He dropped the rifle but held on to the six-gun as he slid down the wall beside the door.

A dark fog clouded his eyes for a moment, then he heard the second man screaming.

"Don't shoot! I didn't draw. For Christ's sake, don't shoot me."

Canyon's eyes cleared and he saw his six-gun was aimed almost directly at the third man, who had stood from the table where he had been sitting. His hands reached over his head.

"God, you killed them both. Just don't shoot me. I hardly know these two guys. Hey, you're hit. Let me help you."

Canyon looked down at the pool of blood beside his right thigh and let the six-gun lower. "Yes, stop the blood and I won't kill you," he said. The dark cloud was coming in again and blotting out his vision for a few seconds.

"I'm coming over there. My gun is on the table. Look, you see it? I got some old towels over here and some clean cloths. You ain't gonna kill me, are you?"

"Come on, I need you. I won't kill you. Stop the damn blood!"

9

"Come on," Canyon bellowed at the only one of the three men in the cabin still alive. "Get over here and stop the bleeding. Tie something around it."

The man came quickly then. Canyon lowered the six-gun and the man put a pad over the wound on the back of his leg where the bullet had slammed through the agent's flesh. He tied the pad over the wound with two wraps of a torn-up towel and kept it securely in place.

The bleeding stopped and the hurting started. Canyon gritted his teeth and stared at the man. He was slight, maybe five-four, had brown hair and a kindly face. He didn't seem to be the killer type.

"Were you with the other two when they killed the governor?" Canyon asked.

The man looked up and nodded. "Yeah, but they didn't tell me what they were going to do. They wanted me to stop the governor and ask directions, then they came up behind him . . ." He stopped and looked away.

"And hit him with a two-by-four?"

The man stared at Canyon in surprise. "How could you know that?" He shook his head. "Willy, the tall one, must have hit the governor twenty times, smashed in his head something terrible. Then they made me drive the buggy sitting right there beside the body. They led my horse and we went up to the Dead Man's Turn they called it."

"Who were they?"

"Willy is from around here. Hasn't been working much. The other one was called Jeremiah, but he just got into town yesterday."

"So it was Willy's idea?"

"Yeah, said he was getting paid. Offered us fifty dollars each. Hell, I been broke for two months."

"What's your name?"

"Skinner, Sly Skinner."

"Looks like your supper is starting to get hot over there, Sly."

"Can I . . . You want me to finish it?"

"Up to you. First, drag those two bodies outside. I don't like looking at them. Don't try running off. You do and you won't be hard to find; then I'll have to kill you."

Sly looked at him, nodded, grabbed one of the men by the shoulders, and dragged him out of the cabin, then the second one. He came back inside at once.

"I'm not exactly hungry," Sly said.

"How far is it to town?" Canyon asked.

"Fifteen miles."

"Why did Willy shoot the buggy horse?"

"They tried to get the horse to go over the side, but she wouldn't. Smart horse. So they drove her right up beside the edge and shot her with a rifle. She fell over the side and dragged the buggy with her."

"Figured. Got any rope in here?"

Sly brought a ten-foot-long piece of quarter-inch rope. Canyon used his boot knife and cut the line in half. "Go over to that bunk and tie your ankles together. I'll check the knots."

Sly did so.

Canyon gritted his teeth and stood up for the first time since he'd been shot. He almost passed out. It hurt like fire to walk on his right leg, but he made it to the bunk. He put Sly's hands in front of him and tied them together with one turn around them and one solid square knot. Then he looped the ends around Sly's back and tied them together there.

"You try to get away and I'll shoot first, understand?"

Sly nodded.

Canyon went back to the stove, put the coffee on to boil, and looked at the skillet full of sliced potatoes and onions that had been frying.

Suddenly he was hungry. He found three eggs, built up the fire, finished the potatoes, then pushed them aside and broke three eggs in the middle of the skillet. He flipped them over, and when they were done, he ate out of the skillet at the raw wood table. The coffee made him feel better. He drank three cups, then a glass of water from the water pail, and shook out two blankets. It was getting cold already. He stood near the fire a minute without putting any pressure on his right leg.

Then he walked normally to the bunk farthest from Sly and lay down. Those few steps had hurt worse than any time he'd been shot in the past year. But he didn't limp a stick. He couldn't show Sly how much he was hurting.

"Get to sleep, Sly. I'm leaving the light on to check on you. Just stay here tonight and we'll see what we can do for you with the sheriff tomorrow." Canyon waited a minute. "Oh, did Willy say who hired him to kill the governor?"

"Sure, some politician named Forester who wants the territorial governor's job."

"You're sure?"

"Yep. He mentioned the name two or three times. We weren't supposed to go into town for three more days, until things cooled down a little. Then we were supposed to get the other half of our money."

"How much was Willy getting?"

"Five hundred dollars."

"Willy didn't work cheap. Good night, Sly."

Canyon had early developed the knack of waking up when he wanted to. It was not much after seven o'clock when he went to sleep and he came awake promptly at midnight, as he wanted to. He rousted Sly out of bed, untied him, and told him what they were going to do.

"Damn, but that will be a surprise for him," Sly said. He had not tried to get away and made no move now.

Canyon partly saw the reason as they got the horses out: Sly was not much of a horseman. They tied the two dead men over their saddles, binding their hands and feet together under the horse's belly. Then they mounted.

Canyon had done all this grimacing with pain. Why did his damn leg hurt so much? He'd been shot before. Sly had put on a new pad and a new bandage around his pants leg before they left just after twelve-thirty.

"You best see a doctor about that leg," Sly said.

Canyon figured it would be a four-hour ride at night, but the moon was out bright and full. Sly knew the way and they cut off some miles going cross-country. They got to town before daylight and Canyon tore down a broadside poster on a store wall and wrote on the back with a stub pencil from his pocket. The words said:

> Forester. Here are your two killers. They aren't as quick as before. You just saved $250. Why don't you do your own killing after this? The third man you hired for the job is in jail.

He tied the sign around Willy's back and tied both the horses with their corpses to the door of the adobe building where Forester had his office.

There was no one up at the jail, but Canyon pounded on the door until someone woke up and opened it.

"Have a prisoner for you," Canyon growled. "He's one of the three men who murdered the governor. Take good care of him. If he accidentally dies in jail, I'll come gunning for you with a shotgun, understood?"

The deputy had seen Canyon around the jail. He nodded, took Sly into the jail, and put him in a cell by himself. When Canyon saw Sly properly positioned, he hurried out of the sheriff's office and jail and left his horse in front of the hotel.

Upstairs, he found Room 214 still empty, so he crashed there and slept without taking his boots off. It was just after five-thirty.

Somebody rattled his doorknob about seven, but Canyon decided not to wake up. He couldn't remember ever being so sleepy. When he heard someone pounding on his door the next time, he sat up and yelled at them. Then he lifted his six-gun and walked to the door.

He moved the chair, unlocked the door, and opened it an inch. He pushed the muzzle through the opening. "What the hell you want?"

"It's me, Deputy Carson, Mr. Canyon. The sheriff says he wants to see you right away."

Canyon opened the door and lowered the weapon. "Yeah, I bet he does. He's got to wait. What time is it?"

"Just after nine, sir."

"Tell him I'll be over to see him as soon as I have a talk with Doc Holtzman."

"You get shot, Mr. Canyon?"

"No. I stubbed my toe and bit myself." Canyon slammed the door, washed his face in the bowl of cold water from the stand, and dried off. He looked like hell. He felt like hell. But he wasn't going to tear up his face again shaving in cold water. He combed his hair, slapped on his dusty brown hat, and checked his revolver. Still had five loads.

The next step he took brought a groan. He had forgotten to favor his right leg and it cost him. Once downstairs, he walked to his horse and rode over to the doctor's office.

Inside, the medic looked at him with surprise.

"Hey, I thought you were too fast to get shot yourself. Looks like you caught a good one. Want me to cut your pants off or you want to drop them?"

He dropped them and Holtzman went to work.

"At least the slug went right through," the doctor said. "Tore up some of the muscle on that leg."

"I figured that out, Doc. Just patch me up so I can get back to work."

"At least a week in bed if you know what's best for the leg."

"Not a chance."

"Then I'll be seeing you as often as I am your friend, Paddy. His side has turned bad on him."

"Couldn't have happened to a better guy."

"What do you think about what the legislature did yesterday?"

"Haven't heard."

"They voted to recommend to the president to have Archibald Forester as the new appointed territorial governor."

"You're joking!"

"Not a bit. Passed the resolution yesterday and to-day the letter of recommendation with Senator Jamison's approval started on its way to the White House on the morning stage."

"I don't believe this." Canyon shook his head. Would Forester go so far so he could be governor?

Holtzman finished the bandage and looked up. "Don't matter much if we believe; they did do it."

"Doesn't seem possible. Can I pull up my pants now?"

Five minutes later, Canyon slid down from his horse in front of the sheriff's office and limped only a little as he walked into the county building.

The sheriff was angry. He looked up as Canyon came in, and stopped writing. He stood, both hands on the desk. "What the hell do you mean bringing in a prisoner and dumping him in my jail without my approval?"

"You said I was a peace officer with jurisdiction here. I'm within all legal requirements."

"I'm releasing the prisoner."

"You do and I'll arrest you myself and throw you in one of your own cells for interference with a federal criminal investigation."

The sheriff took a deep breath. "You'd do that?"

"Damn right. In this case it's justified. That man is one of the three who kidnapped, bludgeoned to death, and then dumped Governor Taggart's body over the cliff. The governor had splinters from a sawn piece of lumber such as a two-by-four embedded in his skull from the beating that killed him. Doctor Holtzman found them yesterday. What more do you want? Charge Sly as an accessory to murder."

Sheriff Parrish sat down and shook his head. "Damn! I guess I have to. All the evidence. Gonna be hell to pay. Why did they kill the governor?"

"Haven't you questioned the prisoner?"

"No, too damn mad."

"He said he was lured by somebody named Willy. Willy didn't even tell Sly what was happening until it was over."

"I'll talk to him. You know anything about two dead men we found tied over their horses and tied in front of Archibald Forester's office this morning?"

"Should I?"

"Figured they were the other two who killed the governor. Showed up about the same time you did. Forester is mad as hell."

"Maybe he should be mad. I don't feel so good myself."

"Got winged, I see."

"I'll live."

"Dammit, Canyon. Ever since you showed up here, people have been dying, you realize that? We had a nice quiet little town, then you came."

Canyon stood and stared hard at the lawman. "I wasn't the one who murdered the territorial governor, you remember that, Sheriff. I don't care if you get reelected here or not. You better stop thinking about that and find out who hired Sly and his two friends to kill the governor. That's your job." Canyon put on his hat and walked out of the office and to the street.

He was starved. He rode the block up to the café and walked in. Jill had a hot cup of coffee waiting for him at his regular stool on the end.

"Breakfast, I bet," she said.

He nodded. "Lots of everything. I'm starved and mad and about ready to do something stupid. Slow me down at least."

"I'll make you clean up your plate," she said, and hurried off.

He was thinking about going directly to Forester and arresting him for murder, charging him and throwing him into jail. He wanted to, but he knew that would not be a good move. There was too much here he didn't understand.

The damn senator. Why was he fussing around here in New Mexico Territory? Did the professor fit into it anywhere? He seemed to know a lot about what happened in the territory. Forester was the huge question mark. He seemed to fall all over himself doing stupid things that could tie him in with murder and attempted killings. Was the man trying to get himself killed or hung, or was he just stupid?

Canyon started eating automatically when Jill brought the food. He hardly noticed what it was. It was good and he made small talk with Jill as he worked out his battle plan. He soaked the last bite of a stack of hotcakes in the warm maple syrup and chewed it.

"A fine breakfast," he said. "Give my compliments to your chef."

"I did the whole thing," Jill said.

He stood and kissed her on both cheeks. "Try to see you tonight," he said, and hurried out the door. For the moment he didn't notice his leg. But as he walked toward the hotel, he felt the pangs, then the steady drumroll of pain as it lanced into his head.

He slowed and favored the leg with a small limp. He walked directly to the second floor and to Room 236. There was a note on the door: "Miss Jamison has returned to the governor's house and will be staying there for the next few days."

Canyon rode his horse to the mansion, three blocks away, and went around to the kitchen entrance. Two women worked in the kitchen preparing late breakfasts. He talked to one of them and she nodded and hurried away.

She was back in a minute or two and motioned for him to follow her. They went up a back stairway and down a carpeted hall to the second door. The cook knocked and then hurried away.

Elyse came to the door, opened it a crack, and when she saw Canyon, she pulled the door wide and hurried him inside, then closed the door and threw the bolt.

"I couldn't believe it. I don't know why you're here, but you are. I'm feeling ever so much better about my

. . . relations with men. Can we pick up where we left off the other night?''

"No. We have to talk."

"Oh, damn, that sounds serious. Why are men always so damned serious?''

"Because they have to be. I want to know exactly why your father is so interested in New Mexico. Surely you know. You must have heard him and his cronies talking. I really need to know.''

"Oh, damn." She whirled away and her short robe twirled around her, exposing her legs almost to her knees. "Supposing that I do know and told you. Then would you be extra special nice to little old Elyse and . . . and pick up where we left off?''

"I think I can guarantee you that, Elyse. Why is your father spending so much time and energy in New Mexico?''

"Politics! I'll never understand it. From what Daddy says, he is in an excellent position to be a power in New Mexico. I'm not sure I know what that means. He has said several times that Governor Taggart was not the right man for the job. It seems to me that the accident Mr. Taggart had was extremely convenient for my father. But what do I know?''

"How does your father hope to benefit from New Mexico? His power is in Iowa.''

"But if a friend of his was territorial governor of New Mexico, perhaps some arrangements could be made. That's about all I've heard. Arrangements about what, I don't know.''

"So the senator wants to be a power in New Mexico Territory, be a power so he could profit from it, but you don't know what kind of arrangements he's planning on making?''

"That's about it. That's all I know. Now, I want you to kiss me the way you did the first time the other night."

"Love to love, but right now I have to see some other people. Room Two-fourteen tonight. You be there and we can see what happens."

"Promise?"

"Promise." He slipped out the door. Now was the time to nail Forester—before he became territorial governor. They couldn't use Sly's words about what Willy said. That was hearsay evidence. They had to find out who hired Willy and use him as the witness. Now, if only the sheriff had kept his word and Sly was still in jail.

U.S. Special Agent Canyon O'Grady hardly felt the daggers of pain from his thigh wound as he hurried out to his horse and rode for the jail.

10

As soon as Canyon hurried into the sheriff's office and jail, he found out that Sly was still in his cell. Then O'Grady had to wait ten minutes to get to see the sheriff.

Parrish looked up, a frown registering.

"Sheriff, I need to question Sly Skinner and I want one of your men there as a witness and who will write down everything that Skinner says."

"Impossible."

"Why? You've got three men sitting out there doing nothing."

"They all have jobs to do."

"Loan me one for an hour, for God's sakes. This is more important."

"Canyon, you are causing me one hell of a lot of trouble and irritation, you know that. Be glad when you clear out of here."

"I feel the same way about you, Sheriff, but I'm trying to do my job."

"Take Carson, he can write."

A few minutes later Carson and Canyon sat in the cell with Sly Skinner. He looked nervous.

"Canyon, I hear you're not with the sheriff. He's

been slamming me around since I got here. I got bruises."

"That true, Carson?"

"I ain't seen nothing," the deputy said.

"I'll do what I can, Sly. Just don't try to escape. Don't go out a door left unlocked, anything like that. Now, what I need to know is who hired Willy to do the job. Some in-between guy. The person you told me the other day didn't stop by the saloon and talk to Willy, right?"

"Oh, no. He wouldn't do that. Let me see, it was at a saloon, the Second Chance Gambling Hall Saloon. Yeah, that was it. They got a big barkeep there who is also the bouncer and keeps a loaded double-barreled shotgun behind the bar. He was the guy who talked to Willy. Yeah, I remember Willy telling me that."

Canyon looked over at Carson. "You have all that written down?"

"Just about."

"I'll wait."

When Carson finished writing on the pad of paper, Canyon pushed it in front of Sly. "Sign it. I'm taking nothing for granted anymore." When Sly had signed it, Canyon had Carson sign it and date it with the time of day as well. Then Canyon signed it and folded the page and put it in his own pocket.

"Thanks, Carson. That's all I'll need you for." They called for the jailer, who let them out.

"Carson, if anything happens to this man, even a black eye, the same thing is going to happen to you. I'll see to it, understand? You better make Sly your personal friend and be his protector, or you'll be hurting damn bad.''

Carson watched O'Grady and frowned. "Damn, I'll try, but I'm not the boss here.''

Canyon turned and walked out of the courthouse and down the street to the Second Chance Gambling Hall Saloon. It was just after eleven o'clock and the place had opened for the morning gambling trade. Canyon went to the bar and soon a man just over six feet tall and broad in the shoulders came out.

"You drinking or looking?'' the apron demanded sourly.

"I'm looking and talking.'' Canyon motioned him down to the end of the bar. When they stood face to face, Canyon made a quick move and his six-gun was out of leather and pushed hard upward under the barkeep's chin in the soft flesh between the bones.

"Move it into the back room, where we won't be bothered,'' Canyon ordered quietly.

The man nodded, his eyes wide in surprise. He backed up through a curtain and into a storage room that also had a cot and a desk.

"Easy with that thing, you crazy?'' the apron asked.

"You better hope I am. I've got some questions. Just how long you keep your face in one piece depends on your answers. You understand that?''

"Yes.''

"Remember what a forty-five slug does as it goes through the top of your mouth and out through your skull. Now, a few days ago you talked to a man named Willy about doing a job, some night work, some killing work. Don't deny it; I know you did and have witnesses. What I want to know is who told you to hire the man.''

"Don't remember.''

Canyon cocked the six-gun and pressed it harder into the soft under-chin flesh. The sound made the man's nostrils flare and his eyes went wide as the color drained from his face.

"Wait a minute, I might be able to remember. Just a second.''

"You've used up your second. You know Willy killed the governor, don't you? That's what you hired him for, so you're part of the group to be tried for murder.''

"Hell, no! You can't—''

Canyon pushed the six-gun harder into the soft skin and tissue under the apron's chin.

"What's your name?''

"Gerb Gosse.''

"Now, who told you to hire this man?''

"I remember now. His name is Del Rumwalt, a security guard for the governor. Little guy with a mustache, about thirty. Gave me ten bucks to send him a good man who could do a dirty job.''

"That makes you a killer, too, Gosse. Don't try to leave town. The sheriff will be around to see you before long.''

"But I didn't know.''

"Hell, don't matter. Where does this Rumwalt work?''

"At the governor's mansion. He's second in charge of the guards there.''

Canyon lowered the six-gun and put the muzzle against Gosse's chest. "I should pull the trigger right now and save the county the cost of another trial. You killed a man, so you deserve to die." O'Grady watched the man's face go white again and his eyes wild. At last the agent let the hammer down gently with his thumb.

"Hell, the courts need to have something to do." He turned and walked out of the room, across the saloon, and hurried down the street toward the mansion one more time. It wasn't until he was halfway there that he remembered his horse and then the pain hit him in the leg again and he limped the last block.

He asked the guard near the front gate where he might find Del Rumwalt.

"Del isn't working today. Somebody said he was home sick."

"You know where he lives?"

"Right down the block from me. Green house with white trim half-block down from Sierra Street on Second. Can't miss it."

Canyon didn't. A knock on the door brought a quick response. A woman with an anxious expression opened the door.

"Good morning, I'm looking for Mr. Rumwalt."

"He isn't here. You probably can find him at work. He's on the security force at the legislature and at the governor's mansion."

"Then he went to work this morning?"

"Surely did. I thought he might be coming home. One of our boys has took sick."

"If I find him, I'll tell him what you said."

Canyon turned and walked away. They couldn't be this efficient. Whoever wanted the governor killed must have used a broad sweeping sword to make sure a trail could not be traced. So where was Del Rumwalt? If he wasn't home and wasn't at work, that could mean he was drunk in some saloon.

Canyon stopped by at four saloons, but nobody by the name "Rumwalt" was in any of them. Just after noon, Canyon checked with the sheriff. He was out, but Deputy Carson was there.

"How is our prisoner, Deputy?"

"Just fine, Mr. Canyon. He's in a single cell and I have given orders that no one opens it but me."

"Good. What do you know about Del Rumwalt?"

Deputy Carson looked up quickly. "Damn, how did you find out so fast? We just found his body at the edge of town a half-hour ago. He's over at the undertaker's with a bullet in the back of his head."

"Damn!"

"So he really does fit into the conspiracy and the death of Governor Taggart," the deputy said.

"He did, until somebody erased him from the chain of the murder. He was an important link and now he's gone. What in hell are we dealing with here?"

Canyon went to the café and had dinner. Jill brought him the special of the day and he hardly noticed her at first because he was concentrating so hard on his problem.

He was out of leads. Sly to the barkeep to Rumwalt was the only solid lead he had that could produce courtroom kind of evidence. Sure, Forester had the trigger pulled, but now Canyon didn't have one shred of solid proof he could take to trial. He was in a box canyon.

Jill sat across from him and frowned. "Hey, I'm sorry you're hurting. Anything I can do to help?" She smiled. "Maybe a woman's viewpoint on it would help. Sometimes we think different than you men do."

He looked up and nodded. "Thanks, Jill, but right now I don't see how anything can help me. I probably should just get on the stage and ride out of town."

"That's probably exactly what the men who killed the governor want you to do."

Canyon looked up quickly. "Yes, they are trying to counter every move I make. It's almost like they know what I'm going to do next. How in hell can they know that?"

"Who seems to know what you're thinking and planning?" Jill asked.

"There's the sheriff, the doctor, the professor, you, and maybe . . ." He stopped. "Okay, maybe we're not finished here yet. One more faint possibility, tentative straw to grasp at."

He stood, kissed Jill on the cheek, and hurried out of the café. His leg was feeling better. He hardly limped at all now and he made good time getting to the back door of the governor's mansion. He knocked and one of the cooks answered. It was the younger one, the same one he had talked to earlier.

She grinned. "Yeah, the redhead lover. She said to send you right up anytime you called. You know the way."

Canyon took the steps carefully. Lifting the right leg that high caused him sudden stabs of pain. He saw no one in the long hall, so he stepped up to the second door on the right and knocked. It opened almost at once and Elyse moved back, smiling broadly.

"Oh, I just hoped and prayed that you would come again."

He bent and kissed her lips and led her to the bed. She sat, then flopped backward and held out her arms. He lifted her up and kissed her again softly, then looked at her sternly.

"Elyse, I'm in real trouble and you're the only one who can help me. You know the governor is dead. But you may not know that three men killed him and pushed his buggy over the cliff."

He waited a moment, but she lifted her brows in her only reaction.

"I've been around powerful men too long to let something like this surprise me. These men try to get what they want any way they can."

"I know who did it, but I can't prove it. What I need from you is any good reason your father is spending so much time in the territory. You said before he might benefit in some way. I can't figure out how. Any more ideas for me?"

"I might have, but you're going to have to cooperate with me. First get up and bolt the door."

He stared at her for a moment, then did so and returned and sat beside her. She leaned toward him and he kissed her, his tongue darting into her mouth, his arms around her tightly crushing her breasts against his chest. She moaned in delight and battled back with her own tongue. Elyse sighed softly, leaned back, and stared at him with adoration in her eyes. Her hands went to her blouse and the buttons. Slowly she began opening the fasteners.

"I was serious about starting where we left off," she said. "As I remember, I was all bare on top." She shrugged out of the blouse and lifted a short chemise off over her head and let her breasts swing out.

Canyon sucked in a breath.

"Wonderful, beautiful," he said, his own emotions surging.

She moved her shoulders a little so her breasts shook. "Give my ladies a kiss hello," Elyse said softly.

Canyon bent and kissed each perfect orb with small nipples and broad bands of pink areolae. His mouth toyed with them, teased them, worked up and down the sides as she writhed and gasped in his arms. Her hands stroked his hair, tangled in its luxuriant red strands.

"Oh, Canyon, that's so wonderful. It makes me feel like melting and . . . and lying down.

"Now, while I can still think straight, let me answer your question. I'm not sure what Daddy has in mind for New Mexico. I know he has extensive land holdings in two other territories that he helped sponsor. Maybe he wants to buy some land cheap or get a land grant for a railroad. I'm not sure. But one thing about my Daddy: he isn't here in New Mexico Territory just to help the people out of the goodness of his heart. Daddy always has some kind of a deal working."

She put her hand on Canyon's crotch, then felt higher and grinned. "So you're just a little affected by kissing my titties. Good, I'm so wanting you I'm almost undone."

She rubbed his growing erection, then opened his fly and worked a hand inside.

"I don't know what else I can tell you and your wonderful, hard, glorious maleness here about Daddy. Let's see. I know Daddy hasn't liked Governor Taggart since the day he was first appointed. Daddy said he

105

was the wrong man for the job. I'm not sure he fully trusts Archibald Forester either, but he seems to be working with him. Daddy was most responsible for getting Forester named as the legislature's candidate to the president as the new territorial governor. I don't like him. He caught me in the cloakroom yesterday and got his hands all over my breasts. I hit him in the crotch with my fist and he limped away blue in the face."

She pulled out Canyon's sturdy manhood and sighed again, then bent and kissed him along one side, over the tip, and down the other side. She trembled and moaned in anticipation. For just a moment she hesitated at the tip, then continued.

She looked up at him. "Right now I feel so close to you, so involved. Right now I'll gladly do anything you want me to do. Wonderful Canyon O'Grady, I mean anything. I want you, Canyon, I want you right now. I want to feel your body hard against mine and see you sucking on my breasts, feel you lancing deep inside me, feel your touch, bring your own body to the peak of its pleasure. I'll do anything you want me to do, Canyon O'Grady."

Slowly she lowered her head and let his manhood slip smoothly into her mouth.

11

Canyon O'Grady let her hold him awhile in her mouth, then gently lifted her away and lay her back on the bed. She moaned softly and her eyes watched him with love shining from them. He ministered to her breasts, kissing them, licking them, tweaking the growing nipples until she moaned. He had almost brought her to a climax.

She shivered and stared wide-eyed at him, then caught hold of her emotions; he kissed her gently and she smiled as she hummed softly.

He moved away from her breasts and worked his hands under her skirt. She looked at him sharply, but he kissed her again and her objections melted as she smiled.

"Anything . . . you . . . want!"

He pulled her skirt down slowly, taking the two petticoats with it until her bloomers showed. He left the bloomers on and snaked the outer garments away and tossed them on the floor.

"Oh, dear. I just lost my skirt . . . and I don't care. Canyon, kiss me again."

He did, washing her mouth with his tongue, caressing her big breasts with gentle insistence. Her hands rubbed his chest, then reached for his maleness and caught it; she smiled, then moaned softly and closed her eyes as she smiled.

Canyon kissed her lips again, trailed kisses down her neck to her breasts, and smothered them with more kisses and nibbles at her standing tall nipples. He abandoned her mounds, working down Elyse's flat little belly to the tops of her bloomers.

She gasped as he worked lower. Her hands came down to stop him, but he kissed them and took one down to his crotch. He kissed around her bloomers, soft cotton with bows and ribbons on them. Gently he spread her legs and with his hands worked up and down the inside of her thighs to the bloomers, then past, touching her through the cloth. "Oh, God, Canyon. I don't think I can stand . . . this!"

She sat up and hugged him, caught him around his back, and brought him down on top of her on the bed. He kissed her lips again and then her eyes and chin.

"So good . . . I'm so hot I can hardly feel anything else."

He caught the edge of her bloomers and worked them down slowly, kissing her lips whenever she protested.

A moment later they were down to her ankles and she kicked them off.

"Oh, Lord, I'm naked. But I love it. Anything, Canyon O'Grady, anything at all I can do for you."

He spread her legs again and worked his hands up her white pristine thighs almost to her tangle of protection, then went down again. Twice she nearly climaxed.

"Oh, yes. Oh, yes. Darling, more, more!"

He brushed his fingers across her swollen lips, large, red, and so moist they dripped juices on his hands.

"Darling?" she asked. "Please, right now. Please!"

He bent and kissed her heartland, edging her nether lips, and she let out a wail.

"Oh, God, touch me there again," she breathed, almost too faint for him to hear. "Stroke me there! Yes!" Elyse slammed into a climax that drilled her through and through. When she finished, he was caressing her crotch, spreading her nether lips and touching the small clit above.

She watched him solemnly, then pulled him over top of her and guided his erection toward her treasured spot. "Please, right now," she pleaded.

She sat up and pulled at his clothes. She tore buttons off, threw his shirt in the corner, ripped at his pants. He pulled off his boots and a moment later he was naked and lying beside her. She pulled him over top of her again, relishing the skin-to-skin contact.

"Now, Canyon, make love to me now."

She concentrated on his long, stiff tool then and brought it to the very center of her and pushed him between the wet extended nether lips.

Canyon worked forward gently and to his surprise slid inside her with little friction. She was ready.

"Oh, glory," Elyse whispered. "Glory, glory. Nothing can ever be this marvelous again." She began to hump against him; she had not learned that anywhere, it must be an instinct. He worked against her and she climaxed again.

When she recovered, she blinked tears of joy from her eyes. "Now you, darling. Your turn. I'm way ahead of you." She rose to meet him on each thrust and he made it last, slowing when his passion threatened to overflow, then faster when he cooled. He made it a long process and at last misjudged and slipped over the edge. Then he lifted to his knees and elbows and slammed into her ten times, as hard as he could, edging her upward on the bed. The next eight times he exploded and showered her with the fruits of the universe as he sailed to the farthest star and came winging back so quickly.

He blew out a long-held breath and collapsed on top of her, sinking them both deep into the featherbed.

Ten minutes later they sat side by side on the edge of the bed, still not dressed, touching and kissing and coming down from a long emotional high.

When she could talk at last, she spoke after a sweet, gentle kiss. "I've never been so thrilled and glorified and made to feel so extremely special in my life. I'll never forget this afternoon, not if I live to be two hundred."

Canyon chuckled. "At two hundred I hope we can both still make love like that. That was great, just fantastic." He kissed her again, then began to dress.

"You have to go?"

"Yes, I better. I promise to be back sometime later."

"Oh, I hope so. I'd walk across a fire barefoot for you right now, Canyon."

"Don't let it get around. I'm not a popular guy in town at the moment."

"They don't know about you what I know."

Canyon grinned. "And you better not tell them." They both laughed and then he kissed her again. "You be careful and be a good hostess. I'll see you later."

She clung to him a moment, then patted his crotch gently and let him go. Canyon looked past the just-opened door along the long hall and saw two men standing about halfway down talking. He closed the door and waited a minute. When he opened Elyse's door the next time, the two men were gone. He slipped quickly to the back stairs and out through the kitchen.

Land. So the Senator was a land-grabber. How could he do it? A grant would have to go through Congress. Lots of people there would investigate and take a careful look at any such land. He wasn't building a railroad, so there was no chance the senator could get a railroad land grant like some of the lines got in the East.

Canyon walked to the newspaper office and this time talked to the editor, a small man with a humpback and a nervous tic. His name was Melvin Knightswood.

"Land-grab? Sure every territory has to fight against that. The laws governing land are a lot less lax in a territory, especially when dealing with one as sparsely settled as New Mexico. I've heard some men have become millionaires grabbing land out from under the noses of the citizens and the local politicians."

"How can they manage that?"

"A couple of ways. One is to set up a dummy corporation that's nonprofit and dedicated to the welfare of a tribe of Indians. There might be two or three of that tribe left, and the crooks buy them off for a hundred dollars and the nonprofit corporation has expenses that you wouldn't believe. They pay their president a million dollars a year, for instance. All legal. Of course, first they have to get the land grant rammed through Congress."

"Why would anyone in Congress vote for something like that?" Canyon asked.

"Lots of reasons. Maybe a payback for a past favor by another congressman. You owe me a vote, I want it on this bill of mine. Happens all the time. Especially a bill concerned with a territory where there isn't anyone in Congress to protect the rights of the people of that territory. News of these private bills almost never gets much publicity. I take the Washington paper, but by the time it gets here, it's a week old. What can one small paper like mine do anyway?"

"You can do a lot, Mr. Knightswood. You can do a lot. What do you have on the death of the governor?"

"A lot of rumors, not much else. Some say it was murder."

"It certainly was. I know who had him killed, but I can't prove it. You heard that Del Rumwalt got himself killed this morning? He could have been my star witness, but not anymore. At least four men have died so far as the aftermath of that killing, and there probably will be more."

"How do you know it was murder?"

Briefly Canyon told him the facts. "Right now we've got one witness, but so far we can't tie him in with the man behind the whole thing."

"Can I quote you?'

"No. Then I'd be dead next. Talk to the sheriff and see how much of this he'll tell you. I'm still working on the land grab as the motive behind this. Evidently the wrong man was the territorial governor. When is your next issue?"

"Thursday morning. I've got a day yet to get the story."

"Don't quote me, not even as an unidentified source. Might be another week before it's cleared up."
Canyon asked if he could leave by the back door and the editor/printer said he could.

Land-grab. Now it was starting to make more sense. The senator would be the man in Congress to launch a bill and get someone in the House of Representatives to sponsor a similar bill there. What did they want? Where was the chunk of New Mexico that they coveted?

Canyon wished he could get into the senator's room at the governor's mansion. He might have taken some notes, or left some papers around that would spell out the target. But it would be too dangerous for him to burglarize the room. He thought for a minute and then grinned.

It wouldn't be dangerous at all for Elyse to see what she could find. He knew exactly what to promise her for a reward.

Back at the hotel, Canyon checked with the clerk, reminding him that he was still registered in Room 214. The clerk nodded, took six dollars in payment for rent, and handed him three messages from his key box.

The first was from Elyse and had arrived that morning early. He put it in his pocket and looked at the other two. One was from the professor, asking about a chess game this afternoon.

The third note was unsigned.

"Canyon. If you really want to find out what happened to Governor Taggart, meet me at the Palace of Governors building at dusk today the 17th."

Canyon looked at a calendar behind the hotel desk.

This was the seventeenth. The unsigned note could reveal an important piece of information, but it sounded more like a simple way to trap him into a spot for his execution. He'd have to think about that one.

For now he turned and walked back toward the professor's house. As he went, he tried to remember where he had left Cormac. He should be put back in the livery. He remembered a half-block later, rode the big palomino stallion to the livery, and fed and groomed him and then hurried to the Offenhauser's place.

The old man met Canyon at the door. "Good, good. I was watching for you out the window. Now we'll find out if your inquiring mind is just as adept at the intricacies of the master's game of chess. After all, chess is simply classical warfare in the privacy of one's own study."

"Professor, I'm sure I'm not nearly in your class, but this will be a chance for you to totally humiliate me. I do this every so often. It's good for my humility and builds character. In fact, I've built my character this way countless times."

The professor simply nodded and led the way to the carved ivory and onyx chess set that was already set up.

His first year in Washington in the service Canyon had been fascinated with chess and played every chance he got. There were a lot of excellent players there and soon he found some semibeginners he could trade moves with. Gradually he moved up in class, but too often he was off on an assignment so he couldn't get in any real competition.

His books on chess strategy and various classical

openings were long forgotten. Canyon settled down to the board, won the whites on the selection, and made his first move with queen's pawn two spaces forward.

The game ended suddenly twenty-three minutes later. The victorious professor made some notes in a small tablet, including the time and the opponent.

"I like to keep track," he said. "That way I can judge when an opponent is getting too good for me. It would have been a close game except for those two moves."

Canyon laughed. "Those two moves were master blunders. It's been too long since I've played. To lose a queen and a rook in two moves is a game-ending blunder."

"Another game?" Offenhauser asked.

"I'm not ready for two such disastrous defeats in an hour. Let me think about my mistakes for a while. Perhaps tomorrow."

"Your mind isn't on the game. I hear you're working with the sheriff."

"Yes, I somehow got involved. Actually through a boyhood friend who is in town I hadn't seen in ten or fifteen years."

"I hear a rumor that the governor was murdered," the old professor said.

"Must be the same one I heard."

"Those two dead men tied to Archibald Forester's front door have me stumped. They must have been intended for him. The other two men with offices there are not politically involved."

"It's a mystery to me, Professor. Do you think the governor was killed for political purposes?"

"Now you're getting into my field. He's a politician,

so it must have been political. The question is, which politics? I haven't a clue and I've been thinking on it.''

"Professor, if a local expert like you has no idea, I have no business trying to figure it out. Best thing for me to do is get on the next stage and get back East, where I belong.''

"Well, now, that doesn't make us sound sociable at all. Say, did I notice a slight limp when you came down the street?''

"Just a scratch. Oh, you might be able to help me with this. I went in to buy a newspaper and the editor got to talking about Governor Taggart. He said he'd heard about the murder rumor, too, and figured it all might have something to do with what he called a land-grab. He told me in some territories politicians have been getting huge grants of apparently worthless land for charities, then keeping the land for themselves. Then the politicos benefit from the land. Have you ever heard of anything like that?''

"Indeed I haven't, Mr. Canyon. I suppose it could happen, but such a bill would have to get through both houses of Congress and that doesn't seem likely. Most bills of that sort get a highly critical evaluation by the congressmen.''

"Well, I guess I'm grasping at straws. The drowning-man syndrome I imagine. I've wasted enough of your time. I think I've recovered well enough from my humiliation at getting so soundly thrashed that I can hold my head up long enough to eat supper.''

"Your play was fine, O'Grady. With a little practice

we could have some rousingly fierce battles, I'm sure. I'll look forward to our next contest.''

Canyon said good-bye and went to the door. He closed it softly but all the way down the walk to the street he had one jittery feeling that the professor was staring at him in a malevolent fashion. He couldn't shake off the shivers for another block.

He had more than an hour until dusk. Would he go to the grand old Palace of Governors that the Spanish had built back in 1610? He had decided there would be no information given, but the mere fact that somebody was going to be there to try to kill him just might lead back to someone else who could be a part of the conspiracy.

But would he live to find out who that could be? If he were going, he should be there an hour ahead of time, which meant now.

Was he going or wasn't he?

He turned and walked toward the ancient building. He knew he was going. There was not a chance that he would let a challenge like this go uncontested.

He got there over an hour before dusk and found what he wanted, a spot near the palace that was a little higher than the rest and gave him a good view of most of the front of the old building. He settled down behind some bushes and shrubs and waited. Canyon knew he would have felt better if he had the Spencer carbine, but it was too late for that now.

Less than half an hour after he arrived, he saw two men slip into the area and talk briefly. Each had a rifle. One went to the north side of the front of the old building and hid in a doorway just around from a corner. The second one found a spot that would give them a cross fire, and settled down behind a stack of split stove wood.

Then they waited.

Canyon decided on the one by the woodpile. He was closer and there was a concealed route so Canyon could get behind the bushwhacker. He bent over and walked quickly down a faint trail through some brush and then cut to the left past a building and came up just behind the man shielded by the woodpile.

Canyon moved cautiously now, making sure the man in the far doorway couldn't see him either, and worked up behind the woodpile man. It took him ten minutes of cautious movement to get into position.

Then he ran out of concealment. There was nothing but dry, hard-packed dirt between him and the man behind the big pile of split wood. This whole area was now shielded by the cord of wood so the other bushwhacker couldn't see Canyon. But if the bushwhacker by the woodpile turned around, he couldn't help but see Canyon. He took the chance. He bent over low and took cautious steps. The Colt in his right hand had the trigger cocked and ready.

His four-inch hunting knife from his boot now rested in his left hand as he moved along slowly toward the hidden man. His right leg began to pain him where he had been shot and then screamed in protest at the bent-over position he was in. Another few steps.

Canyon was almost there when the hidden man turned and saw him coming. Canyon lifted both the knife and the six-gun and dived at the surprised sniper.

12

Canyon's left hand drove the knife ahead like a spear and he felt the blade bite into flesh. His momentum rammed the four-inch blade into the soft flesh up to the hilt, and the knife slipped from O'Grady's hand as he jolted into the man's body and rolled over top of him.

Canyon came to his knees and pounded the side of his six-gun against the bushwhacker's head. The man made no sound. He slumped to the side.

The U.S. agent pushed the man and looked for his knife. It remained in the man's torso where it had plunged in just under his heart and driven upward. The man was dead. Canyon went through his pockets quickly, found a letter with his name on it, and pushed it into his own pocket. Then he left the same way he had come, circling around the large shape of the old Palace of Governors building to get to the man on the far side.

It took him twenty minutes, but it was nowhere near dusk yet. Again he moved cautiously, watching behind him and to both sides as well as ahead. There could have been a third man he was not aware of. Possible, but he didn't think a third man was there.

He came to the far corner of the palace and bent low to the ground and peered around the adobe blocks. At first he could see little. The doorway where the second shooter had hidden was indented into the wall. Then a moment later Canyon saw a boot slip out past the side of the wall before it was drawn slowly back in.

If Canyon couldn't see the man along the wall, then the bushwhacker couldn't see Canyon. He didn't have to worry about whoever else might be around the palace. He stood, again drew the cleaned boot knife, and edged around the block wall. The doorway was about ten feet along the wall.

Would a shadow give him away? No, the sun was behind the mountains to the west. He moved without a sound on the sunbaked dirt. Six more steps and he was almost at the door. He could see some of the far side of the opening.

Now!

He surged around the corner with both the knife and the gun up. A man slouched there smoking a cigarette. His rifle lay across his legs.

"If you move or make a sound, you're a dead man," Canyon said softly.

The man's eyes went wide. "Where in hell did you come from?"

"I'm the guy you were sent here to kill. Unless you want to be as dead as your friend over there behind the stack of wood, you answer my questions quickly. Who hired you to kill me?"

"Guy in a bar, forget which one."

Canyon slammed the Colt down across the man's head. It cut a furrow across the side of his head and tore his ear. The shooter slumped to the steps and groaned.

"Next time, I'm going to shoot you in the knee. That means you'll never walk right again. Who hired you?"

"Guy named Pete Wallsich."

"You sure that was his name? Describe him."

"About five-eight, broad shoulders, brown hair, and a mustache. Light complexion. I figured he was Irish."

Pete was a name Paddy McNamara had used when he was a kid. He had hated the name "Paddy" then because he got teased about it, so he had used Pete often. The description fit.

"How much?"

"Fifty dollars each."

"How was it to work?"

"Pete was supposed to come about dusk at the main door. When he stepped away and raised his hand, we would shoot your head off."

"Thanks. Is that him coming over there?" When the man looked where Canyon pointed, the agent slammed his six-gun butt down on the man's head, knocking him unconscious. He tied him and gagged him and left him in place.

Then Canyon picked a place where he could be out of sight and be much closer to the main doorway, and waited.

Just as it was getting dusk a figure came out of the gloom and looked around. He saw the big doors and walked toward them. At the doors he waited a minute. Canyon wasn't sure if the man was Paddy or not. Had to be.

The agent moved away from his protection, held the

Colt in his hand, and cocked it, then walked toward Paddy.

" 'Evening, Paddy, nice you could come."

The figure turned and started to draw, but saw the gun hand. It was Paddy.

"What's with the shooting iron? I said I wanted to help you."

"Sure, the way you did last time. How's the side?"

"Not the best. Hey, I can tell you lots about the governor's killing."

"Like it was done here in town. Like he was beaten to death with a two-by-four and then driven to the crash site. Like they shot the horse because it wouldn't go over the edge."

"How you know all that?"

"My job, Paddy. How come you're working for a killer?"

"My job." He ducked. "Hey, you see that crazy flying bat? It flew right up there." He lifted his right arm, but nothing happened.

"Didn't see any bat, Paddy."

"You must have, it almost hit me."

Paddy looked around. "Come on, right now, you guys," Paddy screamed, pawing for his own six-gun.

"Don't get it out of leather, Paddy, or you're shot again. I might not be quite so kind this time only to wound you."

Paddy's draw stopped and he bellowed in anger. "What happened?"

"I got here first, Paddy. One of the men is dead, the other one tied up. That wasn't sporting of you, two men with rifles. Weren't you afraid of getting splattered with my bloody brains?"

"You always were a bastard, Canyon."

"True. Now, who told you to kill me? Who are you working for?"

"You can ask that until you die of old age, Canyon."

"We'll see how a murder charge loosens your tongue."

"Murder?"

"That man I had to kill. He worked for you, was on your orders, and died in the operation. So you're as guilty as if you were the killer. It's all in the law books. Try reading them sometime."

"You'll never convict me. Not in this town."

"Just swear that you work for Archibald Forester, and that he ordered you to kill me, and that you killed Del Rumwalt on Forester's orders."

"How in hell did you know?" He stopped. "You're bluffing, Canyon. You always did bluff a lot. Also, I bet you don't have the guts to shoot me in the back. I'm walking out of here. If I do what you say, I'm a dead man even if you keep me in jail. So what do I have to lose? I'm gambling that you can't shoot down your old friend with a slug in the back."

Paddy turned, stared over his shoulder at Canyon in the almost darkness, and walked away six steps; then he ran, zigzagging away until he was out of sight in the dark.

Canyon watched him go and eased the hammer down on the full chamber. No loss. He knew where Paddy lived and could pick him up almost anytime. He hadn't denied he worked for Forester, which was some progress.

It took Canyon nearly a half-hour to get the tied-up

man down to the jail and throw him in a cell and tell the sheriff about the body behind the woodpile. Someone had just reported it as well. The sheriff looked unhappy, growling about another damn killing, and had Canyon write out a statement and sign it.

When he was done, he went to the café and eased down on his favorite stool at the counter. He sat there a minute and no one came. He looked around and saw Jill standing near the back with her arms folded and sporting a frown.

He motioned to her. "Could I have a cup of coffee, please."

Reluctantly she went to the coffeepot and poured him one and took it to where he sat.

"Haven't seen you for a while. Haven't seen you at my house for days."

"I've been busy getting shot at."

"Just dandy, go ahead and get yourself killed. I made a fool of myself for nothing."

Canyon looked up. "I don't remember anyone making a fool of herself. I remember some tender moments."

"Moments. Sure. Takes a hell of a lot of them to make up a life, and I ain't been having enough of them." She watched him a minute, her frown fading. "Oh, damn. You're doing it again, just being here. Reckon that you want some supper."

"If there's a special of the evening."

"Bought me another quarter of venison off Earl. You want a steak?"

"Be fine. I'll pay."

She stood close to him and shook her head. "Canyon O'Grady, around here you don't pay for nothing.

Ain't you figured that out yet?'' She harumphed and walked back to the kitchen. Tonight there was no other waitress on duty.

As he sipped his coffee waiting for the steak to fry, he tried to put the pieces together. Evidently a land-grab was arranged, mostly in Washington, D.C., so why did they have to eliminate the territorial governor? Did the governor have to approve the deal? Not if it was a bill through Congress. Would he be in a position to argue against it if he knew about it? Yes, that sounded more realistic.

Such a deal had to be done quickly and quietly. A territorial governor in the halls of Congress talking against a bill that was going to affect his territory adversely certainly wouldn't be something the people behind this wanted.

So, Forester was one of the wheelers, but what about Senator Jamison? Canyon had no definite evidence against him. He had been traveling with the governor. His daughter said he had some land in other territories, but that could be legitimate. When it came right down to evidence, Canyon had none against the senator, and not even any sound suspicions. Could someone be using the senator? Didn't seem likely, but possible.

The steak came and Jill sat with him and had some coffee between times she waited on other customers. It wasn't a busy night.

"Sorry I was such a bitch. It's just that I miss you so much when you're not around. And I really miss you in back, in bed. You going to get shot at tonight?"

He grinned and said he could use some sleep instead of charging around on a horse all night.

"Can't make any promises, but I'll try. I've got to go see the newspaper man. This is Wednesday, so he'll be getting the paper set up and printed."

The steak was great, and so was the rest of the meal. Canyon insisted on paying a dollar for it and walked down to the newspaper, but he took the back alleys and watched carefully before he slipped in the unlocked back door of the newspaper.

Melvin Knightswood was working over a case of type busily picking up each individual letter and putting it in a line of type.

"Good evening, Mr. Knightswood," Canyon said.

The hunchbacked man glanced at him, smiled, and went back to work.

"Door was unlocked, so I came in," Canyon said. "Looks like you're running a little behind schedule. You should be on the press by now."

Knightswood laughed. "Tell me something I am not totally unaware of, Mr. O'Grady. But since you're here, you can help. Hand me that galley of type on that metal tray. If you drop it, I'll kill you."

Canyon passed over the hundreds of individual letters that had been formed into words and sentences. The tray was two inches wide and about two feet long. Setting type for a newspaper was a backbreaking, mind-sapping job.

Knightswood finished arranging the type, tightened it into place in the galley, and used a soft wooden mallet against a piece of soft pine to tamp the letters down so all of them were the same height. Then he spread ink over the tray of type with a rubber roller, put down a long strip of newsprint paper, and pulled a heavy roller over the type that was held solidly in place.

Knightswood stripped the proof off and handed it to Canyon. "Make yourself useful and read this to catch any misspelled words or bad grammar. I got to get the back pages printed."

"What else do you know about Senator Jamison? I hear he has property in three of the newer territories."

"Free country. Own property anywhere a man wants to."

"Also heard he might have come by it in some kind of swindle, a land-grab."

"I heard the same thing, but can't confirm it."

"You cover the legislature, too?" Canyon asked.

"Yep."

"Why would it be important to a land-grab scheme to have the right man in the governor's office?"

"Congress consults with local officials, especially the governor, to check out the request, the integrity of the people involved, the size and location of the grant, et cetera. An honest governor would have to be bribed—or murdered."

"That certainly fills in a hole in my logic. Thanks. Now I'll read this." Canyon got through the story and two more small ones, found only one wrongly spelled word and one mistake in number, and marked them with a pencil. He gave the proof to the newsman, who grunted.

"Damn, been spelling that word wrong for thirty years. Think I'd learn by now." He loosened the type, took out the offending line and corrected the spelling, and then repaired the second mistake and bound the type back together.

"What do you know about Archibald Forester?" Canyon asked.

"Damn good politician: smooth, talks good, greets and meets better'n any preacher, a master at working to the good side of folks. Also as dishonest as a night rider, a rogue, a bastard I wouldn't want near my daughter, and a number-one enemy of the common man."

"You seem to have built up quite a liking for the man."

"Never done a thing to me. Always answers my questions, gives me news stories when they favor him. But I don't trust him. If he's in link with Senator Jamison, this territory could be in for big trouble."

"Forester isn't territorial governor yet."

"And should never be. But the senator's weight is going to weigh on President Buchanan's decision about whom to appoint here."

"I've heard about Forester for only a few days, but my dislike for him is starting to catch up to yours," O'Grady said.

They moved back to the press, one of the older ones where a sheet of paper was laid on the flatbed of the press and a long arm was brought down and leaned on to give the proper pressure to print a sharp image. Then the lever was lifted, the printed sheet removed, the type inked by hand and a new sheet of paper put down. Then the lever and its heavy weight was lowered again and pressed tightly to print another sheet.

"Want me to swing the lever for you for a couple of hundred times?" Canyon asked.

"Sure, but why should you?"

"I've put in some time in a newspaper shop. This

is the worst damn job around except putting type back in the case."

"You're on," Knightswood said. "But don't complain that I didn't warn you."

Canyon took off his vest, rolled up his sleeves, and put down his hat, then he went to work. "How many copies are you printing tonight?" he asked.

"Three hundred," Knightswood said. "You're lucky, last week it was three-fifty."

Canyon yelped and swung down on the lever.

"That's two," Canyon said. "How many pages?"

"Only six pages, that's a thousand eight hundred strokes with the lever." The editor laughed at Canyon's expression.

13

After the first three hundred sheets had been printed on the newspaper, Canyon wanted to beg off, but he considered the time and how long it would take the printer to do the next fifteen hundred pages all by himself, and relented.

"Where's the new page?" Canyon growled. "We better get moving or we'll be here all night."

Knightswood looked up and grinned. He lifted the second heavy page form into the flatbed, got it adjusted and leveled down, and the printing process began again.

Canyon crawled into the bed beside Jill just after two A.M.

She awoke and kissed him. "Where have you been?"

He told her.

"At least nobody was shooting at you." At once she began to seduce him and it was another hour before they got to sleep.

After breakfast the next morning, Canyon prowled the town. He wanted to talk to the lieutenant governor, one of the other four men appointed by the president. Maybe the sheriff would know where he lived.

Canyon was on his way there when a buggy with side curtains pulled up beside him.

"Canyon," a woman's voice called. He went over to the rig and found Elyse motioning to him. "Get in, let's go for a ride."

He stepped into the buggy and she drove them down the street and out of town on the north road.

"I love it out in the country, even high dry land like this," she said. "It's so much more interesting than the city."

"And we can be alone," Canyon said, knowing what she was getting at.

At once she pulled the rig to the side of the trail and reached out and kissed him. "Now, what shall we do?" she asked, her eyes sparkling.

"Talk," Canyon said. "Do you know who the lieutenant governor is?"

"No."

"Great. Can I talk frankly about your father?"

"Why not? Everyone else does."

"I mean, you won't get mad at me and make me walk back to town?"

"Not if you kiss me enough."

"I'll try." Canyon kissed her and gently caressed one of her full breasts. "I think your father is up to something sneaky here. I don't know if it's illegal, but it could be. I think he's trying to work some kind of a land-grab."

"He's been accused of that before."

"Did he do it before?"

"Well, yes, I think so. I don't pay much attention to those things." This time she kissed him and pushed one hand down to his crotch and began feeling around.

"He could get in big trouble this time. I think the sheriff is looking into it. Maybe you can help your father."

She laughed. "That will be something new. He's always so self-sufficient. Usually he doesn't even know I'm around, except when he wants me to put on a low-cut dress and charm his friends at a party or a dinner."

-"And you love it."

"True. But how can I help him here?"

"Just poke around his desk or where he keeps his papers on this trip. See if there's anything about a Senate bill to make a land grant to any small group of Indians. It would really be a big help."

"Help to you, or to my father?"

"Both of us, if I'm right. Could you do that for me?" He kissed her again and worked one hand through the buttons on her blouse and found a bare breast. She sighed and then kissed him with her mouth open. When the long kiss was over, he felt the heat from her breast.

She nodded. "Sure, I can take a look. He doesn't carry many papers with him. Says he leaves the paperwork in Washington for his secretaries."

"Think you could get a look at them this morning?"

"No. I'm going to be making love to you all morning."

He gave her breast one more squeeze and then pulled his hand free. "I'm afraid not, sweet Elyse. I've got an appointment with the sheriff. He gets testy if I'm late. I hope you understand."

"Oh, sure, get me all excited and then drive away. Oh, hell, I'm used to that. I'll see what I can find."

She bent and kissed his fly where his erection was

halfway along. Elyse shook her head and brushed back a tear. "Wish somebody would tell me what I'm doing wrong. I want so much to get some man to love me."

"Hey, you're not doing anything wrong. This time you just picked the wrong man. I can't afford to love any woman, even a beauty like you. I'm a traveling man. Never have stayed in one place long."

"Damn!"

He picked up the reins and got the rig into motion, turned around in the road, and headed back to town.

"You see what you can find in your father's room. Maybe if you don't see anything that looks important, I could have a chance to look through it."

"You're not a spy or anything?"

He chuckled. "Not that I know of."

"Good, 'cause then I couldn't help you." Her hand hadn't left the lump at his fly. "Oh, damn, I wish I had time to play with you. I really get worked up about making love. I've decided there's nothing else I'd rather do than get all naked with you on a nice soft bed and really go at it."

"Soon," he said. "I have these things to get straightened out."

She kissed him again, her mouth open, her tongue charging into his, her hand working hard at his crotch. Then they came into town and she had to ease away from him.

He handed her the reins and stepped down from the buggy near the courthouse.

"I won't let you kiss and run the next time," Elyse whispered to him. "Next time I want you all night."

"Sounds good. You take a look and see what you can find. If it's anything about land in New Mexico, you bring it to me at the little saddle shop right down the street there, at noon. Then I'll buy you some dinner. All right?''

Elyse nodded. Canyon stepped back and watched her drive off, then he walked toward the sheriff's office. He didn't have an appointment, but he wanted to see if the sheriff would swear out a warrant for the arrest of Archibald Forester for murder. He had two witnesses—well, just one actually in custody.

Sheriff Parrish grinned when Canyon walked in.

''You're up early for a man who causes so many killings,'' the sheriff said. ''Have another body for me?''

''Not a one. Want to talk to you about charging Archibald Forester with murder.''

''Be fine if we had any evidence. One of your witnesses died. Your other one don't know a thing about Forester, all hearsay. Fact is, a lawyer came around this morning and said I had to let both of them two men go that you jailed. Not enough evidence, especially on the one last night.''

''You released them?''

''Had to. This lawyer said he'd get a writ after me and a court order. I don't want no trouble with the judge.''

''You can't just let a prisoner go. You have to wait for a court order or bail to be set.''

Sheriff Parrish stood and adjusted his gun belt. ''Son, don't tell me in my jail what I can and can't do. I'm the one the people elected here, not you. You have any more harebrained ideas about the law, you better go see a judge yourself. Now I've got some work to do.''

Canyon stormed out of the courthouse, slapping his

hat against his leg. He had to hit something. The sheriff had actually released the two men he'd put behind bars. Absolutely crazy!

A woman with a young child by the hand stared at Canyon as he hit his leg with his hat again. He shook his head and creased the headpiece and put it back on. What the sheriff did could be considered a criminal act. He'd have to check, but he was sure. He could file charges with the court. But first he'd wait and see what else happened.

Maybe if he followed the senator himself for a while, it would turn up something. He walked out to the governor's mansion and asked the guards at the gate.

"The senator told us he'd be at the territory house most of the day talking with the legislature," one of the guards said.

Canyon turned and walked in that direction. After asking several people in the wooden building, he discovered that the senator was in conference with the territorial land commission and would be there until noon.

Maybe he could stir up something else. He found out where Archibald Forester's office was. He was a territorial representative. He was in his office between sessions of the body. A lanky young man with a strange grin questioned Canyon in the outer office.

"Just why do you wish to see Mr. Forester, Mr. O'Grady? He's an extremely busy man these days."

"Just tell him that Canyon O'Grady wants to see him. I don't think there'll be any trouble."

When the smirking young man went to the first door to the right behind him and opened it, Canyon was right behind him, pushing the youngster forward into

Forester's room. It was large, well-furnished. A woman sat in the chair beside Forester's desk in earnest conversation.

Forester looked up, saw his aide and then Canyon's shock of red hair, and stood at once. "Well, this is a pleasure. Canyon O'Grady, I do believe. I've heard a lot about you, glad you at last came to see me." He looked down at the woman. "Mrs. Waithright, I'll be in touch with you about your situation. In the next week or so. Now, if you'll excuse us . . ."

She rose, nodded, and walked out the door.

The aide remained. "Sir, he simply burst in, I couldn't stop him."

"Yes, Harley, I understand. Now Mr. O'Grady and I have important things to discuss. Don't disturb us, please."

Harley lifted his brows in surprise and hurried from the room. Forester remained standing. He was half a head shorter than Canyon. His soft demeanor changed.

"I don't like what you've been saying about me, O'Grady," he growled. "Don't like it in the least."

"That's too bad, Forester. I don't like the way you order men to kill me. Right now you should be in jail on murder charges—the only problem is both of my witnesses have conveniently been killed."

"Are you accusing me of murder?"

"I most certainly am. I know it, you know it, Sly Skinner knows it unless you've killed him by now as well. I'm here to warn you, Forester, that you'll never be territorial governor of New Mexico, and you'll never own a square mile of the land that you're working so damn hard to grab."

Forester couldn't control his surprise.

Canyon knew that he'd hit a nerve. He plowed on. "Yes, I know about the land swindle. Know almost all about it. Just a few more pieces of the puzzle to fill in and then both you and the senator will be in prison for a long, long time. No, you might not ever see prison, just a jail until your scrawny little body stretches a hemp over a trapdoor as you get hung for murder."

Forester sat down hard in his chair. "I . . . I don't know what you're talking about. But be aware there are laws against slandering a man. If you say what you just said in front of three or more people, I'll have you in court so fast—"

"It's only slander if it isn't true. I won't have any trouble proving it is. I just thought I should warn you. Now would be a good time to cut your losses and get out. You're a smart-enough politician to know about leaving a sinking ship, Forester. I'm not sure if your partner is quite that smart. But maybe he is. I just learned that he has large sections of land in three other territories."

"Get out, Canyon. Don't ever come to this office again. Lies, all of it, lies. I don't have the slightest idea what you're talking about."

"Let me spell it out a little better. You hired the man who shotgunned my hotel room. He missed, I caught him coming off the roof, then one of your men killed him with a rifle. You hired Del Rumwalt to hire three men to kill Governor Taggart. I killed two of the three in a shoot-out in your cabin near the mountains. I brought Sly back and now the sheriff has released him. I wouldn't value his health for a minute.

"Then you hired Paddy McNamara to take care of

me for good. His plan failed too and he's about ready to tell everything he knows.''

Canyon watched the smaller man carefully, but he made no move for his desk drawer. ''Just thought I'd give you something to think about, Forester. You could have had a promising career. Too bad you tried to speed up the normal timetable.''

Canyon turned and walked out of the man's office, past the surprised aide, and into the hall. He figured that Forester would do something. Just what, he wasn't sure. He must have heard a lot of things he only feared that Canyon knew. How would he try to protect himself?

Canyon went outside, covered up his red hair with his low-crowned hat, crossed the street, and entered a small store. He watched out the front window and soon saw Archibald Forester hurry out the door of the house and wait impatiently at the street. Soon a buggy rolled up with Harley driving, and Forester stepped in.

They turned toward him and Canyon let them pass, then took to the street walking after the rig. He didn't think it would be a long trip. When the buggy got half a block ahead, Canyon used his Indian trot and kept the rig well within range. It made two turns, traveled about five blocks, and came up in front of the neat white boardinghouse where Paddy McNamara stayed. Forester got out and went in, and Harley drove the rig down a block, turned around, came back, and parked three houses down.

Five minutes later Forester came out of the boardinghouse and Harley drove to pick him up, then the buggy returned by a different route to the parking lot behind the territory building.

Now the frightened man would be reporting Canyon's accusations to Senator Jamison. He'd like to sit in a quiet corner and listen to that conversation. He pulled out his Waterbury. He had only ten minutes to get to the saddle shop; Elyse might show up.

He arrived at the leather store and went in. The smell of the fresh leather and the dyes and the tanning odors created a wonderland for him. If he ever had time, he dreamed of making saddles and other fine leather goods. He loved to work with leather, he just never had enough time.

He watched the man working on a saddle.

"Sorry, I don't need anything, just like to stop in and smell the leather. Many people do that?"

"Some. I get so used to it I forget what it smells like. Sometimes, first thing in the morning, I get a whiff of it and remember. How about a handmade saddle tailored to your exact seat and weight? Makes a big difference riding. You're a big man, probably never got a saddle that's right for you."

Canyon nodded. "That's for damn sure, but I'm just passing through."

He saw Elyse drive up in her buggy and he hurried outside and got in. She drove away and parked down the street in front of a vacant lot.

"Well, I'm a real traitor now. I found some things I didn't want to find." She handed him an envelope. Inside was a printed copy of proposed U.S. Senate Bill 4819: "a land grant to the Imnahu Indians of New Mexico."

"It's all there. How he has a companion bill introduced in the House and how he needs the endorsement of the New Mexico legislature or the territorial governor to present to the Lands Commission in Washington.

"We stopped by to see the Imnahu Indians. There

139

are only eight of them left in a small settlement high in the Sangre de Cristo Range. The five men are in their fifties, barely alive, and the three old women are worse off. In a year there won't be any tribe left.''

''And in case the tribe dies out, the tract goes to the Jamison Nonprofit Corporation for supervision and advisement, or some such fancy term,'' Canyon filled in.

He saw tears in her eyes. ''He's stealing the land he gets given to them. The grant is for forty sections. That's over fourteen thousand acres. I don't see how he can do this.''

''Elyse, I'm sorry. I didn't know how to tell you. Your father is little more than a sophisticated thief. He's using his high office to get rich. I have information that he's done this before in other new territories.''

Her eyes went wide. ''My God, you're right. I never realized what he was doing, and I . . . I guess I helped him.''

''You didn't know what he was doing. Don't blame yourself. Please don't let on that we know about this. It all should be over in a day or two. Elyse, I work for the U.S. government, directly for President Buchanan. I'll try to do this as painlessly as possible for you.''

''That's impossible. You've already used me. Now take your evidence and get out of my buggy. I'm getting away from here as fast as I can. There's a stage out tomorrow, heading for Independence. From there I can get to St. Louis and a train back to Washington. I don't know what I'll do then. Right now, I really don't care much.'' She reached in and kissed his lips gently. ''Good-bye, handsome man. I wish we'd had more time together.''

14

After a feeble wave good-bye out of the buggy, Elyse drove down the street. That was the end of Canyon's pipeline of information about Senator Jamison.

Canyon headed for the café. It would pay to give Jill some consistent attention. Surely she'd be in a good mood again after last night's party time.

When he got there, he found Sheriff Parrish coming out the café's door.

"Canyon. Good. I was just starting to look for you. You know the woman who runs the café here?"

"Yes, we're friends."

"Must be. She's been kidnapped and they left a note addressed to you. I read it . . . my job." He pushed a piece of paper toward Canyon.

"Kidnapped? You sure. Why would anybody want—"

"Read the note."

Canyon read:

> To Canyon O'Grady. Your girlfriend is gone. We have her, and if you ever want to see her alive again, you'll ride out of town to that same little cabin in the mountains where you met Sly, and you'll bring fifty thousand dollars. There are twelve of us and we're

covered all the way. If you don't bring the money, you both die. Be there by noon tomorrow, August 19th.

"Sheriff, you're a lawman. What do you make of it?"

"Don't rightly know. Plain they must know you don't have fifty thousand dollars and can't get it. Maybe they just want to get you out of town for tomorrow."

"What's happening tomorrow?"

"Nothing special that I know of."

"I have to do something. I can't let a good woman like Jill be cut down in her prime."

"You want a posse?"

"Could you raise one?"

"Probably not. Folks hereabouts don't cotton to going riding off where they might get shot at."

"What I figured. Suggest that you close up the café and send the cook home. That way Jill won't get stolen blind while she's gone."

"I was going to do that," the sheriff said, and went back inside.

Riding time. They must have grabbed her sometime after the breakfast rush. So they couldn't be to the cabin yet. If they were even going out there. But they would need someplace to keep her, and the cabin might be the best spot. Certainly it was far enough out of town so they could stage a battle and not be heard.

Except the only battle they wanted was one rifle round through Canyon's skull. This wasn't a ransom note, it was a trap to eliminate one Canyon O'Grady. Again.

He stopped by at the hardware and bought a box of

142

.52-caliber shells for the Spencer. He had a box of .45 linen-wrapped rounds for his revolver in his saddle-bags. Then he hurried to the livery stable.

He saddled Cormac and went out the back door again, taking his Spencer carbine in the boot. About fourteen miles. He could get there before dark if he hurried. No, he'd have to take a roundabout route in case any bushwhackers were watching the normal route.

He remembered the place and how to get there. He had to go. Sure it was a double-purpose ploy by Jamison and Forester. It would get him out of town for a day, and it would allow the sharpshooters a chance to kill him on a long chase. Only he would show up early and blow them right out of the game. Like getting the first six shots in a shooting contest in the bull's-eye. The other guy had to play catch up.

Canyon rode Cormac hard, working a half-mile to the left of where he knew he had to go, skirting through dense growth of ponderosa pine and the start of the higher-growing Douglas fir. It was an interesting ride, his not knowing if at any moment a sniper's bullet might knock him off the horse.

After two hours he let Cormac take a break near a small mountain stream and drink his fill. He had made good time and figured he was about nine to nine and a half miles toward the cabin. It wasn't much after two-thirty that afternoon when he mounted the big palomino stallion and headed upstream to the ridge he had to go over to get into the next valley and the stream where the cabin sat.

He had no grand strategy, no finely tuned tactics. All he could do was scout the place, watch for people, be sure someone was there, and hope he could see Jill. Then he would figure out what to do. It would be cold tonight, so they would have a fire, at least a cooking fire. He grinned. Yes, even that might work.

For now he rode. He pushed Cormac into a canter down a gradual slope, then eased off when they went to the top of the ridge. It was as he remembered. The pines marched in unison back through the edges of the valley and the hills and ridges for as far as he could see.

There was a fortune up there in saw timber. ''Well, I'll be damned, that's it,'' he said out loud. The golden stallion with white mane and tail looked back at him, and he patted his neck. That must be what Jamison was after. The land could not be farmed and it was worthless for grazing, but here were millions and millions, maybe billions of dollars in saw timber. Senator Jamison figured it might as well be his.

An hour and a half later, Canyon edged into the end of the timber in the valley and saw the cabin ahead as he remembered it. He was downwind, slightly east, and had smelled the wood smoke in the pristine alpine atmosphere for the past hour.

Yes, smoke came out of the chimney. It was a rock-built fireplace from the ground up, as he remembered. He hoped that the kidnappers had left their horses in plain sight. It would make it a lot easier for him to figure out how many were there. He had no idea if Jill could ride a horse. Some women could out here, but most never had tried.

He was about a half-mile from the cabin when he left his horse there, taking the rifle, and moved up through the trees. He checked the sky and figured it was about an hour to dark. Plenty of time for scouting.

He kept downwind so not even the horses would know he was there. The second time he crawled to the edge of the brush he spotted horses behind the cabin tied to a rail. There were four of them. That meant three kidnappers and Jill. He didn't think one man would ride fourteen miles double with the woman if he didn't have to.

Three of them. What next? He saw a pile of wood against the side of the cabin. It would be easy to climb from the wood to the roof and then stuff the chimney with some sacks or a blanket.

When the smoke filled the cabin, it would drive them all outside and he could wait until they were out there and pick them off one at a time. Maybe.

On the other hand they might figure out someone was on the roof and slip out and shoot him full of holes.

Canyon didn't like the idea of storming in, kicking down the door, and shooting it out with them. He'd done it before, but then only his life had been at stake. Now, one of the kidnappers might use Jill as a shield. That option was out.

He worked around through the timber until he could see the back of the cabin. It had, as he remembered, no windows. He could slip up and lead their horses away. That would be his first move after dark. Now he wasn't sure any of them were even in the cabin.

Wait.

He settled down where he could see both the front door and the single window in front and checked his weapons. The screen door banged and he looked up to see a large man with a full black beard come out of the cabin and stretch. He looked at the sun, went around, checked on the horses, and then vanished in the woods a minute.

Probably relieving himself. The man came back adjusting the red suspenders on the denim pants and went back inside.

One man. He had a six-gun on his right hip.

Probably two more. Did they leave any bushwhackers down the trail? He might never know. Depended how well it went after it got dark.

A half-hour later the door opened again and Jill came out. She was not tied. A man behind her laughed as she walked ahead of him. He said something.

"Shut up, you bastard," she screamed at him.

"Just you shut up and piss and let's get back inside."

It was getting dusk. Almost too dark. Canyon had a chance. He picked up the Spencer and sighted in on the man. Less than forty yards away. Fish in a barrel. Then the kidnapper moved in back of Jill. She was directly in the line of fire.

Jill said something and squatted. The man shrieked with laughter and squatted too just out of reach of her, but again the woman provided perfect cover for him. Not a chance for a shot. It would have been easy. Kill the man, not let the two inside come out, and get Jill to bring all four horses over to him.

It seemed to take her forever.

At last she stood and the man behind her got up. Still a chance. He grabbed her and put his hands on her breasts. She tried to slap him. The man guffawed and walked her back to the cabin in lockstep, his hips pumping against her buns all the way.

"Dammit," Canyon whispered as the kidnapper marched her into the cabin. He heard wild laughter and then a scream, and the sounds all stopped.

By that time it was so dusky dark that he could barely make out the cabin. He circled, moved closer, then came up in back of the place and approached the horses slowly. He gathered all four reins. The mounts were still saddled. Without a sound he walked the horses away from the cabin, then into the heavy brush and timber and a quarter of a mile downstream. He tied them securely to the brush and hurried back to the cabin.

When he had gone after the horses, he had seen an old mattress discarded behind the cabin. He slipped back there now and found it ripped open and spilling out matted cotton batting or some such material. He grabbed huge globs of it and threw them on the roof. They landed without a sound. He went around to the side to the woodpile and climbed on it silently, then stepped on the roof. It was like a ladder.

Canyon carried the Spencer with him and now took careful, easy steps across the roof. It was made of sturdy beams and shiplap with shingles. In two trips to the edge of the back roof he had enough of the batting. A good quantity of smoke came from the chimney. He stood and pushed the heavy matting down the chimney in the biggest bunches that would fit. Soon he could stuff it in with his hand and seal it tightly.

He moved to the front edge of the roof, lay down, and held the six-gun in one hand, the Spencer beside him.

"What the hell?" he heard someone shout. Then a

man coughed. A minute later somebody ran outside. Canyon could barely see him in the darkness.

Soon two more men came out, dragging Jill with them.

Canyon shot one of the men holding Jill. The man went down in a heap. He winged the second man to the left, who sprinted for the side of the house and out of sight.

The third man held Jill.

"Don't know who the hell you are, but you throw your six-gun down right now or this little girl is dead meat. I mean it. Don't matter none to me."

"Don't matter none to me, either," Canyon said. "Second she dies, you do too. You want that?"

The man pushed Jill down and scurried backward into the night. Canyon fired three times and his six-gun went dry. He grabbed the Spencer and heard the man laugh.

"Well, now, your stinger done got pulled. Five shots. Let me try some target practice."

Canyon had the Spencer up and ready to fire. He aimed at the sound, and when the first muzzle flash came from the man's six-gun, Canyon fired twice as fast as he could. He aimed just below the muzzle flash and there was no second shot from the kidnapper.

"Jill, don't answer me, just fade back into the brush somewhere. There's one more snake I've got to take care of. Go now."

Canyon slid to the side of the roof, pushed out the brass, and loaded six linen-wrapped rounds into his Colt. It took a while to get the caps in place in the dark and the powder and ball wraps rammed into each cylinder. Then, he held the hammer in the fired position so it couldn't fall and dropped the eight feet to the ground.

He hit hard, went to his knees, then recovered and crouched against the wall. His leg was hurting, but it didn't matter.

"Kidnapper, the only one still alive. You've got two choices: stay here and make it easy for me to kill you, or you can start running due north into the woods; when you get out there about a hundred yards, you can fire one round in the air. You do that and I won't kill you. Take your pick, but do it now."

A moment later Canyon heard someone running through the brush.

"Don't shoot, I'm going. Dammit, just don't shoot!"

Canyon waited until he heard the man's shot well up along the ridge, then he checked the two bodies. Both men were dead. He took their six-guns and then called softly.

"Jill? Jill, where are you?"

She came flying at him from the darkness. He had time to put out his arms and catch her. She was sobbing.

"Oh, are they really gone?" She clung to him, her head on his shoulder. "I've never been so scared in my life. They said as soon as it got dark I had to do each of them four times."

"How many of them, just three?"

"Up here, but they left two men down the trail somewhere. One man came into the café and said you'd been hurt and were asking for me, so I went with him. Then outside in the alley, he put a gag in my mouth, another man tied my hands, and they put me on a horse. We rode through the alleys and out of town. Then we came here.''

''It's all over, we're going back right now. Let's go find the horses.''

She touched his hand, then reached up and kissed his cheek. ''You know, Canyon, this is the first time since I've met you that I can look at you and not want you to make love to me. Right now it just doesn't seem that important.''

''Hey, this lass is growing up,'' Canyon said. He caught her hand and they walked back toward where he had left the four horses and then down to his own. He put lead lines on the three unneeded mounts and trailed them behind his own.

They rode for a mile, then stopped.

''We're well enough hidden now so that last man couldn't find us if he tried. What would you like to do, ride another four hours and get back to town, or rest here and ride in tomorrow morning?''

''Let's stay here. I'm still sore from riding out here. We can keep warm together. I want you to hold me in your arms until I go to sleep. Would that be all right?''

It was.

15

When they rode back into town the next morning, they went through the alleys to Jill's house so that as few people as possible would see them. On the way back he had told her who he was and why he was investigating this whole affair.

"So, what happens now? You can't just go up to a United States senator and accuse him of being a criminal."

"I wish I could. No, you're right, it has to be more involved than that. I need some way to make them work against each other. Maybe a couple of letters that could be delivered to them 'by a friend' might do the trick. Do you have some good writing paper and a couple of pens and ink?"

An hour later, Canyon was still hard at work at the table writing. He had done the letters a half-dozen times to get them just right. Ambiguous enough to hint at a lot more than they said, yet punchy and to the point on certain common elements. He read through the final draft of the letter to Archibald Forester.

Dear Mr. Forester:
You don't need to know who this is, but as a friend,
I felt that it was my duty to you and the territory to
advise you that all is not the way it seems to be with

U.S. Senator Jamison. He is not what he appears to be, and his promises to you are highly overstated. Do you have any agreements from him in writing? If not, I would suggest that you do so at once. Friends in Kansas and Colorado have told me that they no longer have any trust whatsoever in the senator from Iowa.

I'm not saying he will do the same thing here, but in Colorado, he has come into several large land holdings, not as a partner or in conjunction with a non-profit corporation, but as a single owner.

I simply hope that you will be prudent and get in writing any agreements you have with the senator.

I wish I didn't have to write this note to you, but you'll understand it all one of these days. Good luck on your project, and I remain your faithful, if not revealed, friend.

Canyon left the letter unsigned. He read it a last time, decided it would do what he wished. He had to stir up some anger, some jealousy and distrust in the conspirators. He wasn't sure if the senator and Forester were the only ones involved.

He looked at the second letter.

Dear Senator Jamison:

I'm a friend, but I don't want to identify myself. Please take this information and evaluate it; however, I think you'll be surprised what a poor job for you Archibald Forester has done here in Santa Fe.

I in no way stand to gain. I am only thinking of my friendship with you and my wishes for the best for you. However, some elements have come to the forefront which must be considered.

First, Governor Taggart's "accident" was a botched job from the start. Several people around town know that it was no accident, that the men Forester engaged were incompetents who made mistakes from the outset. The general is always responsible for the errors of his troops.

The campaign against the redheaded detective, who I understand now is a federal agent, carried out by Forester has been stupid, poorly thought out, disruptive, and of course nonproductive, since the man still lives and breathes.

This man is your most important problem. No matter what else goes right, this man could bring down your whole house of cards in this territory and others if he is not stopped.

However, even he is not as dangerous right now for you as is Archibald Forester. If he is a partner or participant, he is absolutely the worst choice that could have been made. I am not a purist, but for a sophisticated operation such as this, there must be a lot of thought, planning, and careful execution of the smallest details.

I pray that it is not too late. From my evaluation, Mr. Forester must go if there is to be any success.

I hope you will take this letter in the spirit of friendship and someday you will understand my concern for everyone involved.

Again, the letter was not signed.

Canyon read the second letter again, folded it twice, and put it in a long envelope and then considered how to deliver the two messages. He wanted as few to know about the letters as possible.

Jill finished reading the letter to Jamison. "These are going to make somebody real mad."

"I hope so. Angry enough to blow the partnership apart. I have a feeling these two need each other. Now, how do I deliver them?"

Canyon solved the problem by finding two young boys on the street and giving each of them a quarter to deliver the sealed envelopes directly into the hands of the addressees.

He instructed Jill to stay indoors until sunset. The third kidnapper might be back after his long walk and would report to whoever had hired him.

Canyon returned to the territorial house and positioned himself well down the hallway from Forester's office. He kept on his hat to keep his red hair out of view and remain somewhat less conspicuous. Then he waited for any explosions that might take place.

About three o'clock, he saw Forester come charging out of his office. He had a letter in hand and went striding down the hall away from Canyon. The agent hurried after him, saw the man pause outside a room, and then collect some of his dignity and march into the room. Canyon could guess who was inside.

O'Grady found a niche to lean in as he watched the door. It took nearly half an hour before Forester came charging out of the senator's office. His face was red. His coat was unbuttoned and there was a bruise beginning to show on his cheek. His eyes brimmed over with anger and hatred. He shouted something back inside, then slammed the door.

Canyon walked up quickly and caught Forester by the left arm and hurried him down the hall toward the outside steps.

"See here . . ." Forester began. Then he saw who had hold of him and he wilted.

"Archibald Forester, I am a United States agent working on the orders of the President of the United States and I hereby arrest you for various crimes, including the brutal murder of Governor Taggart. I'm taking you at once to the county jail, where you'll be held for trial."

Forester sagged even more.

"The bastard. He was going to cut me off. I wasn't going to get a dime out of it. I do all the dirty work and give my recommendation to the damn Congress of the United States to get his damn bill through the Senate . . ." Forester frowned and broke off the sentence.

"I know all about it, Forester. The land-grab, the dying Indian tribe, Senate Bill 4819. In fact, I don't think there's anything you can tell me about that swindle that will be news to me."

Forester laughed. "I bet I can. You give me immunity from prosecution and I'll give you dates and names and times and everything you need to put those two bastards right where they deserve to be."

"Those two?"

Forester laughed again. "See, you don't know the whole story yet. Promise that I won't be tried for the swindle and I'll name every name."

This time of day there were rigs for hire in front of the territorial house, and Canyon hailed one, put Forester on board, and got in himself for the short drive to the courthouse.

Once there, he paid the driver and escorted Forester inside.

Sheriff Parrish was the first one to see them come in the door. "What's going on, O'Grady?"

"This man is under arrest. The United States government would appreciate your cooperation in holding him in one of your cells until he can be moved to another jurisdiction or held here for trial."

"I can't do that. I told you I don't believe any of your ranting, Canyon."

The agent's six-gun came out in a fast draw that left the sheriff staring. "Then I'm also arresting you for crimes against the local and federal government." Canyon looked around and saw Deputy Sheriff Carson.

"Carson, get over here and relieve the sheriff of his gun belt and his keys, then make a place for these two federal prisoners in your jail cells."

Carson looked at the sheriff, then at Canyon.

"Come on, Carson, this is a legal order, I'm an agent working for the government. Now move!"

Five minutes later the two men were in cells and Carson had taken over as senior deputy.

"Under no circumstances let either of those men out of their cells," Canyon said. He went back to Forester's cell and pulled up a wooden chair outside it.

"Now, Mr. Forester, you were telling me about the land-grab with Senator Jamison."

"Hell, you probably know most of it. Had the little Indian tribe spotted and primed. They'd agree to anything for a couple of hundred dollars. We get the legislature or the governor's approval. That's why I was going to be the new territorial governor. Then, when we get the land, we hold it for a few years, and it goes into control of a nonprofit corporation as stipulated in the grant. Three of us were the corporation officers, Jamison, me, and Jamison's daughter.

"It's the timber we want. We figure in five years there'll be a railroad in here and then we can saw and ship lumber out of here. Must be fifty million dollars' worth of timber up in those forty square miles of mountains.

"Still nonprofit, mind you, but we can take salaries

as we see fit to run the corporation. A million dollars each a year if we want to, and it's all legal and unbreakable. Almost damn worked.''

"You mentioned a third man," Canyon said.

"True, indeed I did. But before I tell you everything, I want you to get a lawyer in here and draw up an agreement that I won't be prosecuted for the landgrab scheme."

Canyon left, stopped at the first lawyer's office, and brought him back ten minutes later. The agreement was drawn and signed by both parties.

Forester leaned back on his bunk in the small cell. "I said I'd tell you, I didn't say when. You don't need it yet. Get the damn Jamison. Nail the bastard. He said he was throwing me to the wolves. Said I was no good to him anymore. The bastard.''

"So give me some evidence against him. I don't have enough to arrest him.''

"You can charge him with conspiracy, that's enough. I was a lawyer for a while. Get him on conspiracy to defraud the U.S. government.''

"That's an idea. Might shake him up and he'll do something really stupid.'' Canyon stood and went back to the outer office.

Acting Sheriff Carson looked at Canyon. "Can you make the charges stand up in court?''

"Hope so. I'd have enough on Forester if Parrish hadn't let Sly Skinner go.''

"He that important to the case?''

"Sure as hell is. He's about the whole case.''

"Might work out better than you thought." He motioned. "Come down here." They went two doors down along the hall the other way from the jail and the deputy opened the door.

A man sat on a chair by a table eating. When he looked up, Canyon yelped. "Sly Skinner!"

"Yep. He came back in, said too many people were trying to kill him out there. He's been cleaning up the place, mopping out, doing odd jobs, running messages. He's willing to testify. He told me Forester was bound to be arrested sooner or later. He said he'll testify if he can get one of them immunity deals."

Canyon was grinning. "Why the hell not? From what he said all he did was hold the horses. Now we've got Forester. Remember I never promised him immunity on any other charges, just to the land-grab deal. That right, Carson?"

"Sure is, Mr. Canyon."

"Oh, one more thing neither of you might know," Sly said. "Twice I have seen the Sheriff take money from Forester. Parrish promised to 'keep everything in line' for him."

Canyon snorted. "No wonder he wasn't cooperative when I told him why I was staying. Damn. So, that's why Forester knew every move I made.

"You have a district attorney here in the county?" Canyon asked. The deputy said no. "Then we best be getting our charges written up to file with the court. First, though, I think it's time I went to pay a business call on the right honorable United States senator from Iowa."

16

By the time Canyon got back to the territory house, Senator Jamison had left for the day. An aide said he probably was back at the governor's mansion. Canyon walked over there and realized that his leg wound wasn't bothering him at all now. Either it was healing well or he had simply blocked out the pain.

He asked at the front gate to see the senator, and one of the sheriff's guards knocked on the door and talked to someone.

"What's the nature of your visit?" the guard asked.

"I want to talk to him about the Imnahu tribe," Canyon said, figuring that would get his attention. It did. The aide came back and quickly Canyon was inside the mansion waiting in one of the small rooms off the big ballroom.

Senator Jamison hurried in the door with a scowl on his face that turned into surprise.

"You! You're the one they call O'Grady. What the hell do you want?"

"Want? Why, I want you, Senator. I'm a United States government agent working directly for President Buchanan, and I hereby place you under arrest for conspiracy to defraud and U.S. government, and for the murder of Territorial Governor Taggart."

Senator Jamison's face got red before he could say anything. Then he threw his hands in the air and screamed, "What the hell do you mean? Under arrest? I'm a United States senator. I have certain immunity—"

"Not for conspiracy and not for murder, Senator. Now, do you want me to put you in irons or will you come down to the county jail quietly?"

"The county jail, with Sheriff Parrish?"

"That's right. You can be in a cell right beside the sheriff, I arrested him on the same charges."

For a small, unathletic-looking man, the senator moved remarkably fast. He slashed at Canyon with one hand, spun around, and dashed through the door. O'Grady charged after him.

Canyon saw the obstacle, but too late. The senator had sidestepped Elyse, but Canyon couldn't stop and they collided. He did his best to hold her up, but they both tumbled to the floor. His head rested on her soft breasts when they stopped falling.

"And good evening to you too, Mr. O'Grady," Elyse said.

"Looks like you didn't leave town yet," he said.

Her father had bolted out the front door. By the time Canyon got up and helped Elyse to her feet, Senator Jamison was at the street engaging a hack. It went rolling down the dirt street to the north.

When Canyon raced to the street, there was only one cab left and two state representatives had just stepped on board.

Canyon jumped on behind them. They looked up in astonishment.

"No time, gentlemen. I'm a U.S. agent commandeering this vehicle. Driver, follow that hack up there. Don't lose him and it's worth a five-dollar tip. Go!"

At first it seemed that Jamison didn't know where he was going. He raced down one street, turned right and then right again, and then the buggy rolled back the way it had come. Canyon stopped his rig and the two legislators got out still asking questions.

When the chase resumed, Canyon told his driver to surge up beside the other rig, which he did. Canyon put a revolver shot over the top of the senator's buggy and ordered the driver to stop. He slowed, and when he stopped, Jamison bounded out of the rig and ran between two houses.

Canyon surged after him. It couldn't be much of a race, but when Canyon came past the two houses, the senator was nowhere in sight. The agent checked the area quickly, spotted three places where the senator might be hiding. The potato cellar against the house looked like the most promising.

Canyon lifted one of the slant doors of the cellar and laid it back. It was still too dark inside. He lifted the other door and started to look inside just as a shotgun round went off and Canyon ducked.

"What you doing in my fruit cellar, stranger?" a woman's voice demanded.

Canyon rose and looked at her. "I'm a law officer, ma'am, hunting a suspect. You see a man run through here?"

She shook her head. "Only saw you in my cellar."

Just then a horse pounded out of a small barn at the

rear of the lot, and Canyon saw the senator in the saddle.

"My suspect just stole your horse, ma'am. You have another animal in the barn?"

"Yes, I do. Help yourself. But you pay for her if she gets shot or hurt any, y'hear?"

The house sat near the edge of Santa Fe, with nothing but a stretch of meadow and grassland behind it all the way to the foothills. There was no place to hide. Canyon found the horse and threw on a saddle and soon was on the senator's trail.

The man was out of his element now. He was on Canyon's turf, and the contest couldn't last long.

Canyon could see the figure on a horse riding due west for the mountains. The agent mounted and rode after Jamison. There was no need to track him. From the looks of the hoof prints, the senator was pushing the horse as fast as it would go. The average quarter horse can gallop for about a quarter of a mile, maybe a half if they hold back a little. Anything beyond that and the animal could be injured or go down.

Canyon set the bay mare at a steady trot that would cover about six or seven miles an hour and settled in the saddle for the chase. As far as he knew, Jamison had no firearm, unless he had found one in the barn. This would simply be a matter of riding the senator down and bringing him back to jail.

A half-hour later, Canyon had not caught up with the senator. He had changed tactics, let the horse blow, and then moved slower toward a ravine that wound back toward the hills. At one point Jamison and his horse dropped out of sight. Canyon rushed a little faster then until he spotted the rider again working up the gully. What did he hope to gain? He had no weapon, no equipment—only a horse—and he was in the wilderness.

Again Canyon lost him from sight. The agent had closed the gap to about a quarter of a mile now, but he couldn't catch him without endangering his own horse. So he played cat and mouse. This time the rider did not reappear. He was locked in the gully between where Canyon was now and the visible part less than a quarter of a mile ahead. O'Grady moved cautiously toward the first turn in the gully. He was on the rim of the cut in the land that rushing waters had made over the years.

Maybe the senator wasn't as dumb as he looked when it came to the open country. He must have holed up somewhere to try to defend himself. How?

Canyon dismounted and tied his horse, then drew his six-gun and cocked it, and climbed down into the gully and walked forward. The first big turn was just ahead. He came to it cautiously, worked partway up the side of the arroyo, and stared over the edge down into the gully where it turned. He could not see the senator or a horse.

Canyon went over the lip of the ravine and down the other side and back to the bottom. Nothing. He jogged ahead at his Indian trot, watching the gully on both sides. There was little growth in the bottom, where spring rains would rip out any new plant or tree. Brush and some new pine trees grew along the sides and top. But they were not enough for cover of a horse and rider.

Canyon moved slower now. He was halfway through the blind spot. What could the senator be trying? The sides of the gully were dropping as he climbed uphill. Still they were twenty feet over him as he moved along.

Ahead, the gorge narrowed until it was less then fifteen feet on the bottom. He heard something and looked up just as the first small rocks hurtled past him. Then it was almost too late. A rock slide slammed down the steep slope at him, picking up bulk and sand and rocks and soil as it came. He started one way, then dodged a bucket-sized rock and darted the opposite way, outrunning the first of the boulders and looking upward where it had all started.

He saw a horse tied to a tree, and beside it sat Senator Jamison screaming and yelling like a crazy man.

Canyon waited for the last of the rocks to come down, then he picked a different route and climbed up the side of the gully. The lawmaker had not moved. He sat where he was frozen in place. But still he screamed, a devastating bellow of anger and rage and terror.

Canyon got to the top and worked along it toward Jamison. Still he screamed. Canyon put away his weapon and walked up to the senator. At his feet lay a three-foot-long rattlesnake, its head crushed.

Senator Jamison held his arm, which had started to redden. Two fang marks showed plainly in the white flesh.

Canyon grabbed his boot knife and then slapped the senator, who stopped screaming and began to sob.

"I don't want to die. I don't want to die out here in the damn wilderness. Never should have left Washington."

Canyon used the sharp point of his boot knife and cut an inch-long X through both fang marks, then he sucked on each one drawing out blood and, he hoped, the poison. He spit out the mixture and sucked again on both the wounds. When he stopped, he figured he had most of the poison out. Then he spit a dozen times to be sure it was all out of his mouth.

He knew that snake venom didn't move through the bloodstream quickly unless there was strenuous exercise.

"The chase is over, Senator. You know how close to dying you are right now. You better tell me the whole story."

He did, chapter and verse.

When Jamison was through, Canyon nodded. "You'll have to tell the story again when we get back to the courthouse so it can be written down, you understand this?"

The senator nodded. "If I live that long."

Canyon said nothing, helped the senator on his horse, and led the animal along the top of the gully back toward town and where Canyon had left Cormac.

It took them over an hour to get to town. It was just starting to get dark when they came into the courthouse street and left their horses.

Canyon sent a bystander to bring the doctor to the sheriff's office.

They were midway through writing down the senator's confession when the doctor came. Canyon told him to wait.

When it was over and the senator and three witnesses had signed the confession about the land-grab scheme and the killing of Governor Taggart, Canyon motioned for the doctor to come in.

He unwrapped the kerchief from around the fang wounds, checked them, and nodded.

"Yep, looks like you got bit once. It's gonna hurt like hell for a while, swell up some, depending on how much of the poison got sucked out. You should be fine in three or four days. Just don't get a lot of exercise."

The senator scowled. "You mean I'm not going to die?"

" 'Course not. One bite almost never kills a grown man. Oh, it might, if he decided to run ten miles to get home or something. When the fang marks get cut that way and sucked out, it isn't serious at all. Figured you knew that, you being a senator and all."

Jamison swore at the top of his vocal range for two minutes, seldom repeating a word or a phrase. When he finished, he tried to grab the confession.

"You tricked me," he bellowed.

"Not true. You were close to death, I almost shot you down. Didn't trick you at all. You're lucky to be alive. That little old rattler just convinced you that you're mortal. You'll have twenty to fifty years to think about it in some federal prison. Maybe."

The senator looked up with a gleam of hope in his eyes. "You said 'maybe.' I'm always ready to strike a deal, make a compromise, scratch your back. What are we talking about here?"

Canyon chuckled. "Senator, the 'maybe' meant that you might be hung in a month for the murder of the governor. That's the only kind of a deal you're going to make around here."

Deputy Carson took the protesting senator back to his cell. Canyon went down to the far end of the six cells and watched Archibald Forester.

"You hear that? The senator is jailed and charged.

Now, you have anything else to tell me about that mystery man?''

"Why not? No reason he should get off scot-free. Come in close. I want it to be a surprise for him as well as you.''

Forester told Canyon what he had been holding back—in fact, what even the senator didn't know—and five minutes later, Canyon was on his way into the residential section of town to pay a personal and a professional call.

17

Canyon walked up the path from the street and knocked on the front door. It took a few moments for anyone to answer. When it opened, Professor Offenhauser's face lit up with a big smile.

"Oh, yes, it's the chess master. I hope you've come so we can have a good game."

"Yes, Professor, I'm making a new rule that I always have enough time every day to play a game of chess."

They moved into the den and the professor replaced the chess pieces in a game he had been playing against himself.

"A boring game, actually, when you play against yourself. The only way is to use some established attack like the Chesnov and then to see what new ways you can come up with to thwart it. That way it's fair because on a Chesnov attack, both sides know what the power moves will be anyway."

They set up the board and Offenhauser won the right to move first.

As Canyon waited to make his fifth move, he watched the professor.

"I imagine that you heard that Archibald Forester

has been arrested for his part in the governor's murder."

"Yes, I did hear that. Too bad, the boy had a fine future ahead of him if he had only taken his time. He was overly ambitious, wanted everything now. I can tell him that's not the way for a man to live his life."

"What is the way, Professor?"

"A man has to know his capabilities, to strive for the best that he can be, and then be content with what that produces in life for him. To strive for greatness when you're a frog, say, is ridiculous."

"How about striving to be rich?"

"That depends on capabilities, the field. Certainly in the academic field no one gets rich. I'm a good example of that. Comfortable, but not wealthy or ostentatious."

"But even so, wealth at least could be tried for, Professor."

"Yes, for some. Most of us have to accept our station in life, accept the level to which we have developed ourselves and to which we have attained, and then call it enough."

"But it never is enough, is it, Professor? Only recently I learned that Senator Jamison was one of your students at the university. I congratulate you. The senator has done well since his college days."

"He was one of my bright students, but I can't take all of the credit."

"Nor should you take all of the blame."

Offenhauser was about to pick up a chess piece, but his hand stopped in midair.

"Whatever do you mean by that?"

"That I've just arrested Senator Jamison and he's

confessed to the entire conspiracy to commit murder and land fraud against the U.S. government."

"I'm astounded." The professor pulled his hand back. "Well, now, that's going to take some getting used to."

"He named all of the coconspirators in his confession. Of course, he didn't know everyone locally who was involved."

"I'm not amused by this closing game of yours, Mr. O'Grady. Why not just tell me what you have to say?"

"Fair enough. It was Archibald Forester who tied you into the operation, Professor Offenhauser. In fact, he said you first suggested to him that the senator be contacted to set up the nonprofit-corporation scam here the same way he had done in Colorado and Kansas.

"Forester didn't give me all the details, but enough so I'm now arresting you in connection with the murder of Territorial Governor Taggart."

"Impossible! Ridiculous! Outrageous!"

"The same words I thought of when I discovered your involvement, Professor. A man of your position, your intelligence, and your—"

"Poverty is the operative word here, Mr. O'Grady. Stark, unrelenting poverty for a man the community should be treating like a prince. I deserved to be retired with honors and a handsome pension. Truth is, I couldn't get by on my pension if it wasn't for the monthly stipend I receive from my married daughter."

"But murder, Professor?"

"Of course not. It didn't start out that way. I thought we could convince the governor of the rightness of the project. We had him in for a quarter of the proceeds.

Have you seen that timber? All federal lands now, but what an absolute gold mine! Just five years more to live and I could be wealthy beyond my wildest expectations. Now I never will be.''

''At least the others won't either. I've got to take you down to jail now, Professor.''

''Jail? You think I'll ride off somewhere and hide? I'll be here when you want me.''

''No, I'm sorry, the others are in jail; you deserve to be there as well.''

''Can I take the chess board?''

''Of course. But you'll probably have to play by yourself.''

''Let me get a sweater. It looks cool out tonight.''

''Go ahead, Professor.''

The elderly man raised out of the chair with difficulty, stared at Canyon with watery eyes. ''We really have to do this? My family will be devastated.''

''It's far too late now to consider that, Professor.''

He nodded. ''Yes, I agree.'' He turned to the closet in the hall and Canyon walked with him. In the closet he fumbled a minute, then came out with a twin-barreled derringer in his hand.

''I can't go to jail, Mr. O'Grady.'' He hadn't aimed the weapon at Canyon, but the agent didn't have a chance to draw his own revolver.

''That's only going to complicate the matter, make it worse, Professor. Considering your age, I'm certain we can get you a suspended sentence.''

''By now it's not simply a case of what kind of a sentence I would be given,'' the old educator said. He lifted the small weapon with the gaping twin .45-caliber muzzles to the side of his head. ''The string has run out, Mr. O'Grady. The last tune played, the final page of the final chapter has been written. Now I meet my maker."

Canyon lunged toward him across the six feet of space, but the little gun went off and the professor's head slammed to one side.

Blood and bits and pieces of skull and tissue sprayed the wall as Offenhauser slammed against it and slid down to the floor.

Canyon's lunge carried him all the way to the wall and he caught himself with his hands against the partition. He looked down and saw all that was left of the professor, and he blinked back tears. What a terrible finish for a fine and worthwhile life.

Canyon eased away from the wall and realized his hands were wet with blood and tissue and brains. He scrubbed them off on the small carpet and went out of the house and closed the door. He took a deep breath and tried to walk normally to the street. He stumbled and his eyes were too wet to see through. Slowly he got his bearings, blew his nose, and walked around the block. Gradually the shock of the man's sudden death drained away from him. He took a deep breath.

He had one more social call to make.

Canyon hurried then. News traveled fast in Santa Fe. He hoped he would get there soon. When he came to the house, Canyon wasted no time. He walked up to the porch and knocked and heard someone coming.

The woman was in her fifties, short and dumpy. She smiled at him.

"Yes?"

"Paddy McNamara. Does he still stay here?"

"Yes indeed. He's in the room at the top of the stairs in back. Why don't you go right on up?"

Canyon figured that was the only way. He went up the steps softly and saw the room. No other way out. He moved up to the room without making a sound, and listened. He heard someone snoring.

Gently Canyon opened the unlocked door. Inside, it was like a hotel room: one bed, one dresser, two chairs, a washstand, and a window. Paddy lay on the bed fully clothed, his six-gun on his chest.

Canyon eased to the side of the bed and picked up the weapon, then tapped it on Paddy's forehead and put the muzzle against the side of his head.

" 'Morning, Paddy. Your boys never did get that fifty thousand dollars."

Paddy came awake in a second, his eyes rolled to the right to see Canyon. He didn't move.

"Go ahead and shoot, government man. What are you waiting for?"

"Some explanations. You worked for Forester, you set up the kill on the shotgunner on the roof. You set up the kill at the Palace of Governors. You sent the kidnappers. Why didn't you have guts enough to come after me yourself?"

"Easier to hire somebody."

"But they kept missing." Canyon snorted. "Damn, I always did figure you'd end up stretching a rope somewhere."

"And I figured you'd be a damn lawman. So what happens now?"

"You go to jail with the rest of them."

"Not a chance."

"So I just shoot you here?"

173

"You don't have the backbone for that."

"Try reaching for your iron and we'll see."

They stared at each other a long time.

"It can't end this way, Canyon. You owe me."

"What for?"

"Remember that team back in Brooklyn? Those big draft horses running down the street and you tripped and fell and I pulled you out of the way."

"Yeah. But three times in the last week you used up that credit when you tried to have me killed. By now we're more than even."

"Hell, you can't prove anything against me. You want the big guys. You got them. Jury won't even want to listen to me."

"So come on to jail without any trouble. Free board and room for a couple of months, courtesy of the county."

"Yeah, hell, why not?" He looked up. "I get to put my boots on?"

"Long walk without them."

Paddy bent, lifted his boots from the floor to the bed, and then tugged with both hands to get his left boot on first. Canyon watched him as he did.

Someone knocked on the door, which was still open.

"Mrs. Walton," Paddy said.

Canyon looked at her, then her expression caused him to glance quickly back at Paddy. He had an ankle gun just out of the leg leather and was lifting it toward Canyon. The agent's weapon lifted and he fired, then shot again. The first round had missed Paddy's gun hand by an inch, the second cut through Paddy's thumb where it gripped the handle, and slammed the iron out of his hand and halfway across the room.

"Bastard," Paddy roared. He grabbed his smashed-up thumb with his other hand. "Damn but that hurts! You could at least have tried to kill me."

"Not unless I had to. I figured I had three shots before I went for your chest."

Mrs. Walton fainted in the doorway.

A half hour later, Paddy was in jail with his thumb bandaged by the doctor.

"No backbone," Paddy said as he glared at Canyon through the bars. "Give me another five seconds and you'd be dead on the boards up there in my room. I was aiming for your heart, I just didn't get that far."

"That's the difference between you and me, Paddy. You always aimed low and you hit it. I'm hoping for better things."

Canyon left the jail then and walked in the early evening coolness. Tomorrow he would have a long talk with the County Recorder to draw up complaints on the whole team. There were still two for-hire gunmen at large, but they had probably left town that afternoon when they heard about Forester being arrested.

In the morning he'd get a letter off to the telegrapher in Independence, Missouri, and have him wire all the pertinent information to General Wheeler in Washington. He had no idea how much longer he needed to be here to get the legal work done.

As he thought about it he saw a shadow ahead that floated out from the wall of the dry goods store and angled toward him. But there was no danger. This shadow had a narrow waist and the rest of a good womanly figure.

"Hey, Cowboy. You had your supper yet?"

"Matter of fact, I haven't."

"Good, I've been saving the last steak for somebody special, you want to be that customer?" Jill came out of the shadows and caught his hand and he nodded.

She led him down the block to the café and unlocked the front door and they slipped inside, then locked it again.

"Now, about that supper order," she said. Before he could answer she bent and kissed him. "Seasoning," she said and scampered for the kitchen with Canyon right behind her.

A few more days here and he would have a reply back from the mail and telegraph service from Independence. At least he hoped so.

Canyon found a spoon and pounded on the workbench beside the stove.

"Woman, get me some food," he growled.

Jill threw a pot at him which he caught and carried back to her. She watched him.

"Food first," she said.

Canyon grinned. "Yeah, food first."